PUFFIN BOOKS

TRAVELLER'S TALES

The Roberts are Romany Travellers, born and bred. But the traditional pattern of their lives is changing and their treasured right to roam is threatened.

Billy, Prim and Len Roberts are lively and independent-minded children. Through their eyes and adventures, Anthony Masters charts the lives of today's Travellers. Billy must make an important decision about his education, while Prim finds herself questioning her whole future. Len, the youngest, rarely stops to think – always acting first and taking the consequences.

From being moved on by bailiffs, through several temporary homes, and on to the search for a new future in the countryside, Anthony Masters has created a realistic and moving portrait of a family fighting hard to preserve its individuality.

Anthony Masters is the author of numerous books for children. He has worked with Travelling children for many years and their changing lives are the inspiration behind this book. He runs drama and writing workshops and is a regular writer-in-residence in schools and colleges. He is married with three children.

*Also by Anthony Masters*

PLAYING WITH FIRE

# ANTHONY MASTERS

# Travellers' Tales

PUFFIN BOOKS

The Publishers would like to thank Felix de Wolfe
for permission to reprint extracts from Ewan McColl's
'Thirty-foot Trailer' on pages 61 and 69.

PUFFIN BOOKS

Published by the Penguin Group
Penguin Books Ltd, 27 Wrights Lane, London W8 5TZ, England
Penguin Books USA Inc., 375 Hudson Street, New York, New York 10014, USA
Penguin Books Australia Ltd, Ringwood, Victoria, Australia
Penguin Books Canada Ltd, 10 Alcorn Avenue, Toronto, Ontario, Canada M4V 3B2
Penguin Books (NZ) Ltd, 182–190 Wairau Road, Auckland 10, New Zealand

Penguin Books Ltd, Registered Offices: Harmondsworth, Middlesex, England

First published by Blackie and Son Ltd, 1990
Published in Puffin Books 1992
10 9 8 7 6 5 4 3 2 1

Printed in England by Clays Ltd, St Ives plc

# Contents

This book is dedicated to the memory of Jim Bignell, traditional Traveller and my Romany friend. Also to Billy, Toey, Prissie and other Travelling children I've met and worked with over the years including Dickie and Phoebe.

Finally to Martin Maylam and Philip Godliman, brilliant and perceptive teachers with whom I've had the good fortune to work and with whom I've experienced such enthusiasm for Travelling ways.

# 1    *Moving On*

'They'll be coming in the morning.'

Their father stood staring into the pond. The April evening was warm and they could hear a nightjar somewhere in the woods. 'And we're going to make a fight of it this time.'

Len felt a thrill of mixed fear and excitement. There had never been a fight before. What would it be like?

Reuben Roberts turned from looking into the twilit pond. Twelve-year-old Billy, his eldest son, stood up and said, 'I'll fight, Dad.' Billy was not very tall for his age but he was wiry, with a thatch of brown curly hair and a dark weather-beaten face. He wore crumpled jeans and a torn pullover.

'So will I,' said his sister Primrose, who was a year younger. She looked like Billy, but her hair was a kind of hazel colour and her eyes were a soft grey. Her skin was berry brown all the year. Like her two brothers, Prim looked as if she was part of the outside world – part of the windy heathlands on which she had been born.

'I'll really smack 'em,' put in ten-year-old Len.

Reuben grinned. 'No way,' he said. 'You're not getting into this, not any of you.'

'But, Dad—' chorused Billy and Prim.

'I said no way.'

'I'll smack 'em for you,' repeated Len enthusiastically.

Reuben came and stood over him. 'Listen, boy.'

'Yes, Dad?'

'You're staying in the trailer – like Billy and Prim. And if I see so much as a hair of your head, I'll give you the biggest hiding you've ever had. Am I getting through?'

'If it comes to a fight—' Len was eager. He was thinner than his brother and sister – a little scruff with long straight hair and a round, enquiring face and eyes that darted about like tadpoles.

'Am I getting through?' repeated Reuben even more menacingly.

'You're getting through,' gulped Len.

Billy could hear the rain on the roof. It was great – the most reassuring sound in the world to him. But just before he had gone to bed his mother had said, 'You won't hear that no more – not if they put us in a house you won't.'

A house – that would be terrible. The Roberts were Romanies and had lived in a trailer all their lives. In fact they lived in two. One was for sleeping and eating and generally living in; the other was the posh one with Mum's china and silver collections, dozens of hand-coloured photographs of the family and some of the horses, and sofas and chairs that Gran had had and her Gran before her. The trailers were pulled by Dad's truck and Mum's van.

Sometimes people called the Roberts gypsies, but they didn't like that; it reeked of hatred and suspicion. They preferred to be called Travellers, although they were finding travelling very difficult now. At the moment they were camped in an old quarry near Maidstone. There were quite a few other Travellers with them – some relatives – and they had all been living together in the quarry for a few months.

Suppose they did have to go into a house? Billy shut his eyes and saw a big dark building with tiny windows that hardly let in any light at all. He imagined himself lying on a huge, cold bed under a low ceiling. There was hardly any air in the room and he knew he would suffocate. They couldn't live in a house – they'd all die. Die a horrible forgotten death.

Billy sat bolt upright.

'What's up?' His brother was in the bottom bunk.

'Can't sleep.'

'Neither can I.'

'You thinking what I'm thinking?'

'What you thinking?'

'House. Rotten old houses.' There was a sob in Billy's voice which he quickly turned into a cough. But Len had heard him.

'We're not going to a house.'

11

'We might. The council – they'll put us in one.'

'We'll fight.'

'They're stronger than us. Anyway, Dad said we've got to keep in.'

'Try and stop me.'

'He'll belt you.'

'See if I care.'

That was typical of Len; he lived for the day and never looked ahead. Right little scruff, thought Billy. Always in trouble at school; often in trouble at home. But Billy was different. He looked ahead – and didn't like what he saw. All his life the family had made a living scrap metalling, buying and selling junk, sometimes fruiting in the summer. Mum made paper and wooden flowers which she sold from house to house, and Grandad made miniature vardos, the traditional gypsy caravans. All kinds of people from all over came to buy them. But now they had lost their original site on the Romney Marsh. A farmer had let them live there for years, but the land was taken by the council for a sewage works and from last summer they had continuously wandered from place to place, roadside to roadside – always being moved on by the police until they had come to the old quarry. They had been there three months now, and were just getting used to it when the bailiffs came and said they would all have to move on.

'But where to?' Dad had asked them. In each county, the council had made an official site for Travellers to live on with proper lavatories and washing machines in little breeze block buildings. But there were only a few places on these sites. 'Once they're full up,' Dad had told them, 'you have to go on to the next county – and the next. And if they're all full up – you move on to nowhere at all.'

Nowhere at all was the roadsides and woods and quarries – unofficial sites where Travellers were forced to gather, sooner or later to be moved off by bailiffs and police. And now it was happening again.

When Billy was very young his dad had told him about the old days, when there was seasonal work picking hops or fruit, and there was no need for official sites as there was much more common land. Farmers had valued their seasonal labour then – and they'd only moved on from choice.

'For the last time,' Mum had said hopelessly. 'We've got nowhere to go now – but into a house. That's what they'll give us – a dump of a council house at the rough end of some estate.'

Slowly, Billy fell into an uneasy sleep, his brain filled with miserable thoughts. He heard snoring below him. Len was all right; whatever happened, Len slept. He had blind faith in himself and their parents and was always certain it would be all right in the end. Billy wondered what Prim was thinking. She was a mystery sometimes – a bit like Gran who told fortunes from palms and cards and tea leaves.

'We'll never go into a house,' she had told him at supper-time. 'It's not written for us.' But Billy was not so sure.

In his troubled sleep, Billy dreamt of the house. This time it was much bigger and darker, with much smaller windows. In fact they were only slits. And despite the size of the house, the ceilings were so low that they pressed him so hard into the bed that he couldn't breathe. He could hear people laughing outside the house. The laughter was hard and cruel, like when one of the boys at school had called him a pykie and all the other children had surrounded him in a circle. Then he had hit the boy hard on the nose and again in the mouth and there had been blood and tears and punishment. But he could still hear the laughter now, and when he struggled to open his eyes he had a glimpse of Len standing over him, perched on the edge of his bunk. It was Len who was doing the laughing.

'You sound funny,' he said.

'Eh?'

'You were yelling out the ceiling was coming down.'

'Shut up!'

'Shut up yourself. You woke me up.'

'Want a punch in the face then?'

'Any time – you'll get the worst of it.'

That wasn't strictly true. Billy was much bigger and stronger than skinny Len. But Len was fearless and would never give in.

'What's going on?' Mum sounded cross as she climbed out of bed on the other side of the trailer.

'Now you're for it,' hissed Len, jumping down into his bunk and pretending to be asleep.

'It's you who's going to get it,' muttered Billy, pulling the covers over his head.

'What are you two up to?' Mum was a big woman, handsome with black tumbling hair which she was pushing out of her eyes.

'Billy was talking, Mum,' said Len. 'He woke me up.'

'I was talking in me sleep.'

'Why's that, boy?' she asked, her voice gentler.

'I was thinking about tomorrow.'

'And?'

'Going into a house.'

'Going into a house?' Len said contemptuously. 'We're not going into a house. We're going to fight and I'm—'

'Len.' Mum's voice was steel again.

'Yes, Mum?'

'Why don't you shut up?'

'But—'

'And if you don't shut up you'll get no money tomorrow.'

Money – money for sweets, chewing gum, comics – was very important to Len, so he quickly shut up.

'So, Billy—'

'I was thinking—'

'Look, your dad's got a quick temper and I'm afraid for him tomorrow, I'll tell you that straight. But we're not going into no house – and I'll tell you that straight too. If the worst comes to the worst, we can always move in with Auntie Peg at Beckenham.'

15

'On that site with all the concrete?'

'That's an official site.'

'It's awful. It's in the town. There's no trees.'

'Anyway we got up a petition and we're going to give it to the coppers tomorrow. If your dad'll keep quiet long enough. Not that anyone could put their name real proper on that petition. It's only you kids who are educated like.'

Billy knew that his parents placed a good deal of importance on Len, Prim and him going to school. 'You're going to be scribes for the whole family,' she had once told him.

'But if Dad gets into a fight, they'll nick him.'

'He won't,' she said sternly. 'And I won't let you either.'

'We might *have* to fight,' came Len's voice from the lower bunk. 'It might be—'

'Shut up, you,' said Mum and Billy together.

'Here they come,' Billy heard Reuben say as he peered through the trailer window with his brother and sister.

Two police cars and a couple of land-rovers were driving into the quarry. The land-rovers had tow bars. Billy knew that his father had been up very early that morning because he had been half woken, listening to his familiar voice outside and the mutterings of other men, his uncles, his grandad – all engaged on some task that he couldn't fathom out. Just as he was trying to, he went back to sleep.

16

The quarry had about a dozen trailers in it, a large number of trucks and vans – and an equal number of old cars, most of which were gutted shells. Their insides were scattered around into piles of scrap metal. Tyres and wheels were piled into heaps and old doors and other bits of bodywork leant against the sheer sides of the chalk.

But Prim noticed something her brothers hadn't. It wasn't easy to see, for there was a slight mist in the quarry that swathed and snaked amongst the piles of machinery. 'Look!'

'What?' asked Billy fearfully.

'They've taken the wheels off the trailers.'

And sure enough they had. So that was what they were all doing so early in the morning. Was this Dad's idea of a fight? Billy hoped it was.

But Len was obviously disappointed. 'I thought there was going to be a fight,' he said. 'It's not fair.'

Prim looked around her – at the warm tidy trailer. There were a few bits of china and a couple of carved miniature vardos. But in the trailer next door, she knew the precious china, the sparkling glass, the coloured photographs, the carved horses and vardos were all ranged up in perfect order. Would they be broken if the bailiffs came in? Were all their treasures threatened?

There were about six bailiffs and the same amount of policemen. All of them looked very uneasy. One of the policemen had an Alsatian on a lead. It certainly looked as if they meant business.

17

'I hope they don't let that dog off,' said Prim.

'There won't be any need to,' returned Billy. He opened the window so they could hear what the grown-ups were saying.

'You've already been served with an eviction order – and you haven't complied with it,' said one of the men in a suit. 'We are here to enforce that order.'

'We've got a petition,' said Reuben. He was tall and thin with the same dark features that the whole family had. 'Everyone has signed it.' His hair was long and blew around in the wind that was now stirring the bushes in the quarry. He shoved the petition into the man's hands, but he only glanced at it and then handed it back. Reuben stepped back as if he had been slapped, but the group of Travelling men and women around him edged closer.

'This is nothing to do with us,' said the man. He was wearing green wellingtons but was otherwise dressed for a day in his office.

'It's everything to do with you,' replied Reuben uneasily. 'It's a petition.'

'It's our right,' said a tiny old man with a weather-beaten acorn face. This was Jim, Reuben's father.

'You're trespassing on private property.'

'This don't belong to no one,' said Jim in his gravelly voice.

'It belongs to the Local Authority – as well you know. And as you've not complied with the order, it is our duty – and responsibility – to tow you off.'

'You'll find that tricky, sir,' said one of the

Travelling women. She laughed and the other women joined her.

'Really?' The bailiff looked around. Slowly, light dawned, and Billy could see there was real fury in his eyes. 'This is absurd,' he snapped.

'You can't tow 'em off without any wheels, or at least I'd like to see you try,' said Reuben, gaining confidence from the women's laughter.

'Get the wheels back on,' the bailiff ordered.

'No way.'

'Come on – be reasonable,' said one of the other grey-suited men. 'You'll be fined heavily for trespass.'

'We ain't got no money to pay no fines.' The large hunched woman with a stick was smoking a little clay pipe and her face was as dark and weather-beaten as Jim, her husband's.

Go for it, Gran, thought Billy.

'Madam – if you don't pay up, you'll go to prison.'

'Then take me,' she yelled. 'Go on – take me.' There was an answering roar from the women.

'That's it,' said Prim to her brothers. 'Us women got more guts than you men.'

'Oh yeah?' Len squared up to her. 'Want to prove it?'

'Shut up and listen,' snapped Billy.

'Get the wheels back on – *now*!' said the bailiff authoritatively.

Reuben shrugged his shoulders. 'Someone's nicked me tyre wrench,' he said. He turned to one of the policemen. 'Could you investigate that?'

The policeman suppressed a grin. Then his eyes hardened as he looked into the crowd. 'Horace Webster!' he said sharply.

A thick-set young man stepped back on the fringe of the crowd.

'Webster – I want to question you about a theft from Fiveways Service Station. Stay where you are.'

But Horace was already running towards the edge of the quarry. The policeman began to give chase but was stopped by the crowd.

'Let me through.'

Another policeman moved forward, but the Travellers stood their ground.

Reuben turned on them. 'Let the coppers through.'

'He's one of us,' yelled someone.

'You'll not give away your own kind,' shouted a woman.

'If he's done wrong,' said Reuben, 'he'll have to go. I'm not sheltering wrong-doers.' He suddenly stood tall and commanding, looking every inch the leader that he was not.

'Who says?' yelled the same woman. 'Who do you think you are? God Almighty?'

'Go, boy,' said the dog-handler, ignoring the conflict. He patted the Alsatian on the back of the neck, taking off its lead at the same time. It was off, springing round the crowd and over the floor of the quarry to the distant running figure of Horace, who was disappearing into the woods.

As they both vanished from sight Len said, 'I'm not staying in here no more.'

20

'You stay,' snapped Prim.

But he was off through the door before she or Billy could do anything about it.

'Len!'

But he was lost in the general commotion as Prim and Billy ran after him. All was confusion as the police raced towards the woods, followed and hampered by a milling crowd of Travellers.

'We've got to get him,' panted Billy. 'Len'll do something barmy.'

'He's already doing it,' said Prim.

'You leave my dad alone,' yelled Len, running at one of the bailiffs with his head down and his fists flailing. 'You lay off him.' He seemed to have chosen the biggest and the burliest of all the bailiffs, for the man simply picked Len up and held him at arm's length as he kicked and struggled.

'Give him to me,' said Reuben. 'I'm his father.'

The bailiff dumped Len at Reuben's feet and he bent over and cuffed him round the head.

'Stay there.'

Len, at last aware of a conqueror, lay where he was.

'Sorry about that,' said Reuben. 'He's only a kid.'

'That's all right,' replied the bailiff. 'He's got spirit, hasn't he? You must be proud of him.'

Their eyes met – and Reuben grinned. 'Well, I am proud of him. In a way. In another way he's a right little tyke.'

The bailiff grinned too. He was just about to say something when there was a terrible howling from the wood.

'Blimey,' said the bailiff. 'What's happened to the dog?'

Reuben's expression was grim. 'There's traps and snares in them woods – and they're not ours. Although I bet we'll be blamed for them – as usual.' He turned to Prim and Billy. 'Come on, you two. You've done this before.'

The scene in the woods was tragic. The big Alsatian was lying on the ground, its paw in a cruel steel trap. Two policemen were kneeling beside the animal and one of them was stroking its head while it howled plaintively. Of Horace and the other policeman there was no sign. Reuben, Prim, Billy and Len knelt down beside the dog.

'It's one of the big-uns,' said Reuben.

'This your work?' demanded the policeman brusquely.

'Poachers,' muttered Reuben.

'Oh yeah?' The policeman was cynical.

'Take it or leave it – this is poachers' work. But I don't expect you to believe me. And don't do *that*!'

The dog gave an anguished howl and the policeman dropped its paw, which he'd been trying to squeeze out of the trap.

'What the—? *You* got any ideas?'

'Yes we have,' said Billy. 'Shall I go and get the grease, Dad?'

'OK.'

He ran off.

'We've done this before,' said Prim.

'I bet you have,' said the other policeman bitterly. 'Getting a nice fat rabbit out, were we? Or a pheasant?'

'We never—'

But Reuben interrupted her. 'Ignore him, love. He doesn't know our ways. What's the dog's name?'

'Sam,' said the other policeman grudgingly.

'OK, Prim – do your stuff,' said Reuben quietly.

She began to stroke the dog, whispering his name over and over again. 'Sam – dear old Sam. Sam. You'll be all right, my dear.' The dog turned and fastened its eyes on her. 'You'll be all right – my dear Sam.'

A few moments later Billy came leaping back with the grease.

'All right, Billy boy – go ahead.'

Billy began to spread it on the Alsatian's paw, and as he did so Prim kept stroking the dog and saying, 'Come on, my dearie. It's going to be all right. My dear Sam – you're going to be all right.'

The dog-handler looked at her with a new respect in his eyes. 'You've got on the right side of him and all.'

But the other policeman remained unconvinced. 'Don't let them get round you, Derek. You know they're only springing their own traps.'

Len continued to spread the grease gently.

Then Reuben said, 'Prim, take his paw.' She did as

23

she was told, still talking gently and now caressing Sam with her other hand. 'Now pull!'

With a very swift movement she pulled. Sam gave a little whimper and his paw was out. He lay down, panting, and licking at the paw.

'Best carry him back,' said Reuben. 'I reckon that's broken.'

'Well I'll be damned.' They looked up to see that quite a crowd of bailiffs and Travellers had gathered. And one of the bailiffs was gazing at the Roberts in reluctant admiration. 'I've never seen the like of that.'

Reuben and the dog-handler carried Sam through the woods, back into the quarry and into one of the police cars where they gently laid him on the back seat.

'We'll give you another day,' said the chief bailiff and a ragged cheer went up. 'But if you haven't got the wheels back on those caravans by then – we'll have you arrested.'

Billy looked up at his father. He could see that he was beaten.

## 2    City Streets

The girl was crying in the corner of the playground when Prim went over to her.

'What's the matter?'

She looked up suspiciously. 'Who are you?'

'Primrose Roberts.'

'You new or something?'

'Yeah. Been here a week.'

'You a gypsy?'

'A Traveller,' Prim said firmly. She studied the girl carefully, wondering if she was hostile. She'd like a friend – a Gorgio friend. She'd never had one before. 'You a Gorgio?'

'Eh?'

'A Gorgio.'

'And what does that mean?' asked the girl sniffily.

'It means you aren't a Traveller. You're one of them.'

'One of *them*? What do you mean?'

'It means you're just an English girl.'

'Aren't you English?'

'Kind of. But I'm a Romany first. Then English second.'

'You tell fortunes?'

'My Gran does.'

'Then I hate you.' The girl burst into a flood of tears and Prim looked round hurriedly. She didn't want it to look as if she was making the girl cry or the bullies would soon come across. But she did want to find out what she was on about.

'Why do you hate me? I haven't done nothing.' Prim spoke fiercely, pushing her hazel hair out of her eyes. She looked more like her dad than her mum. Tall and thin with a beautiful nut brown skin.

'You fortune tellers!'

'I'm *not* a fortune teller. It's dying out with us.'

'She's Irish,' sobbed the girl.

'Who is?'

'The fortune teller.'

'She's a tinker then. Not a Romany.'

'*I* don't know the difference, *do* I?'

'What did she do – come round the door?'

'No. She's over there. She said she was a gypsy fortune-teller – and she *looks* like a gypsy. It's only you saying she's not.'

Prim decided not to argue. 'What did she say then?'

'She told me I was going to die.'

'That's rubbish.'

'She told me—'

'Then she told you wrong. It's rubbish.'

'And yesterday she told Helen Brandon she was

26

going to be run over by a lorry – and crippled for life.'

'She can't have believed her.'

'She did an' all.'

'I'm going to sort her out.'

The girl stopped crying and seemed to cheer up a bit. 'Are you now?' she said with interest.


Primrose walked across the playground angrily. It had been bad enough having to move into London for a place on an official site, bad enough to be homesick for Kent, bad enough to have to come to this school, with the traffic that roared round it and the graffiti inside it – but far worse to be blamed for doing things she never would do. She'd sort that tinker out all right. On the way she bumped into her brother Billy, who was playing football with some boys. He seemed to have settled in all right, but she knew that he was as homesick for the country as she was.

'Tinker's stitched us up.'

'Yeah? What doing?'

'Fortunes.'

'Blimey.'

'What's going on?' Len ran up, anxious to know what was happening. He looked filthy as usual and his jacket was torn. Mum would go spare.

'Nothing,' said Prim quickly. She didn't want to excite him. Len didn't have any tact.

'Something's up.'

'Get lost. Go back to your game.'

'All right – all right. Don't get your knickers in a twist.' He poked his tongue out at her and ran away.

'Don't get into a fight,' whispered Billy.

'I'm using me tongue,' said Prim. 'It gets more results.'

'Oi, you.'

'Who, me?'

The girl was as dark and swarthy as Prim, but much scruffier and looked really hard.

'I want a word with you.'

'Yeah?'

'You been telling fortunes? Like accidents and death?'

'That's my business.'

'You're upsetting people. Making them cry.'

'Dearie me.' The girl laughed.

'And saying you was a gypsy.'

'Why not?'

'Because gypsies don't tell fortunes like that.'

'Don't they? What *do* they tell then?' She laughed again.

'About money – and voyages – and distant lands – and handsome mush. That kind of thing.'

'Who says?'

'I know. I'm a Romany.'

'Get you. I'll tell what I like.'

'Well, don't say you're a gypsy. You're giving us a bad name.'

'You've already got one – no problem.'

'It's you who gives it.'

'You accusing me?'

'Yeah.'

'You want trouble?'

'No – but I'll have it if I must.'

The girl was squaring up to her now. This is it, thought Prim. I'll have to fight.

Then the bell rang.

'I'll get you,' said the girl.

'You do that,' replied Prim. 'If I don't get you first.'


'It's horrible here.'

'We're lucky to be anywhere.'

Both the Roberts' trailers were parked on a concrete standing, hard up against the arches of a railway bridge. Every half hour or so a train thundered across, drowning all conversation and the Roberts' television set, even when it was turned up loud. On either side of the trailers were a couple of breeze block lavatories and wash-houses. Someone had already nicked the lead from the roof. Ranged up alongside them were another sixteen hard standings, plus wash-houses and lavatories. Concrete surrounded everything and a main road wound its way past, making more noise. You could almost see the fumes standing out in the stale summer heat.

'Mum.'

'Yes, Prim love?'

'Do you like it here?'

'You know I don't.'

'Can't we go somewhere else?'

'You dad's out looking today.'

'And I miss Gran – and Grandad.'

'They're not too happy either. They don't like staying with Uncle Silas – they never have. He's mean.'

'How long have we got to stay here?'

'You sound like Len. Always full of questions.'

They were sitting out on the front step of the caravan, watching the traffic.

'Don't I get any answers?'

'Len doesn't. I've given up trying to answer his.' She stroked her daughter's hair. 'But we're trying – trying to get somewhere.'

'I mean – there's no room for the trucks – or the scrap.'

'The council have given him—'

'It's too small. Too small for all of them. And them chavvies – they got nowhere to play.'

'They're talking about a play scheme.'

'Do-goody social workers. We don't want none of them. We don't want none of them tinkers either.'

'Takes all types.'

'Know what she's been doing?'

'Who?'

'The tinker. She's been going round reading dud fortunes. Scaring the kids. Doom and destruction stuff – and passing herself off as a gypsy. It's not right.'

30

'Takes all types,' her mother repeated. She was staring at a small patch of dusty grass covered in litter.

'You're not listening to me,' accused Prim.

'Sorry. I was just thinking—' Her eyes glazed over again.

'Penny for them?'

'Well – you'll laugh at me, dearest.'

'Try me.'

'Every time I look at that patch of grass – that dirty little patch – I see that field outside Ticehurst. You remember – the one with the stream at the bottom. We used to camp there when you were a kid.'

'I remember it.'

'I keep looking at the grass there – and seeing it.' She wiped a tear from her eye and Prim put her arms round her and kissed her.

'We'll be back in the country soon, Mum.'

'Your dad will go barmy if we're not.' She looked around her miserably. 'We're not a part of all this.' A train roared overhead. When it had gone, she said, 'The boys will go wrong.'

'Wrong?'

'They'll get into gangs – roam the streets.'

'They're far too sensible for that. Look at our Billy boy—'

'Look at our Len—'

Prim burst out laughing and her mother joined her. They both relaxed, although there had been a note of fear in their laughter. Then Prim said, 'We wouldn't meet tinkers in the country.'

31

'Don't brand them,' said her mother with sudden vigour. 'That's the trouble with us Romanies. We know the Gorgios don't think too much of us. But *we* don't think too much of the tinkers. That's what I call passing it on. Don't you see?'

'Yes, Mum. I *do* see. But this girl keeps telling kids they're going to die. And she says she's a gypsy. She'll get us all in trouble. You see if she don't.'

'Oi, Pykie!'

'What?'

Billy turned round. He was in the playground on a rope swing. It was only a strip of tarmac in the park, and he was far too old for it, but there was nowhere else to go. He stopped the swing and looked up. There was a big boy standing in front of him – far too big for him to handle. Billy's heart sank.

'You a gypo?'

'I'm a Traveller. So what?'

'You been going round scaring my sister?'

'No.'

'Well, your sister has.'

'She ain't.'

The boy grabbed him from the swing and lifted him up by his shirt collar. Then he dropped him and Billy sprawled on the ground, choking and gasping.

'Your sister,' said the big boy slowly. 'She's been going round the playground telling kids they're going to die – and it's gonna have to stop.'

'Oh her—'

'Yes, her.'

'That's not my sister.'

'Who is she then?'

'My sister's going to sort her out. She's a tinker.'

'So what? You're all the same – gypos, pykies, tinkers – you're all the same lot.'

'We're *not*.'

'Don't give me that. You sort the little gypsy out. And if you don't – if it happens again – I'm going to fix you good and proper.' He leant on Billy who was still lying on the ground. 'Got it?' he asked, poking at him with his studded boot.

'Got it,' replied Billy quietly.


'Let's go down her place and shut her up.'

'We can't do that.'

'Why not?' Billy was telling Prim what had happened. She was absolutely livid, but no way did she want to go down to the tinkers. 'They're under the motorway,' Billy added. 'Right dump.'

'We'll get beaten up if we go down there.'

'Then what are we going to do? I'll get beaten up anyway if she carries on.'

'We've got to stop her.'

'How?' asked Billy angrily. 'Just how we gonna do it?'

'Let me sleep on it,' said Prim. 'But I don't want Mum or Dad involved. They've got too much on their plates already.'

'They may have to be,' warned Billy grimly. 'If this goes on it'll get out of hand.'

The brick came through the window at about three o'clock in the morning. Reuben was first up to assess the damage, but when he heard sounds of breaking glass all over the site, he was out and down the steps of the trailer in seconds.

'What's going on, Mum?' asked a sleepy, curious Len.

'Brick. Seems there's trouble outside. Your dad's gone to sort it out.'

'Shall I—'

But Len was destined never to finish the sentence. 'You stay where you are, boy,' she shouted fiercely. 'And that means you two as well.'

Billy and Prim staggered out of bed and looked at the shattered window. They could hear shouting outside – and the sound of running footsteps and hurled insults.

'What's going on?' Len kept saying. 'What's happening?'

'Shut up!' Mum yelled. 'You and your darned questions. Haven't we got trouble enough without—'

'But, Mum – who—'

'I said shut up, Len!'

'Hang on.' Prim went over to the brick. 'There's something wrapped round it.'

'Don't touch,' said Mum. 'That's police evidence that is.'

'Yeah?' said Billy. 'They won't get far.'

Ignoring her mother, Prim picked up the brick and took off the piece of paper. Everyone crowded round curiously – including Mum. 'It's a note.'

'Read it,' commanded Mum.

'OK. It says: PYKIE FORTUNE TELLERS – PYKIE TROUBLE MAKERS. There you are,' said Prim rather smugly. 'She's put the blame on us. I'll get her tomorrow.'

The door was flung open and Reuben reappeared. He was angry and out of breath – and even more angry when he read the note. Prim explained and he nearly hit the roof.

'This is just too damn much. Who the hell do they—' But he was interrupted by a knock at the door. Reuben opened it, and on the steps stood Big Bella. She was fifteen, weighed the same in stone, and had the build of an all-in wrestler.

'I know who's done this,' she said in a mild, little girl's voice that belied her great physical strength.

'So do we,' said Billy and Prim while Len looked angrily at them. He hated being left out.

'I was going to get her yesterday,' said Prim. 'But the bell rang.'

Bella smiled a gentle smile. 'Her name's Patsy O'Bryan – and she ain't one of us.'

'Wait a minute,' intervened Mum. 'This won't be solved by violence. Let me talk to her mother.'

'Let me talk to her dad,' snapped Reuben.

'I *said* this won't be solved by violence,' repeated Mum very fiercely.

'Don't worry, love,' said Bella. 'I'll fix her.' She

smiled her innocent smile again and then bid them good-night.

As the door closed and Reuben searched for something to put temporarily over the window, Mum said, 'Prim.'

'Yeah?'

'You can't stand by and see Big Bella hand out one of her beatings.'

'That Patsy deserves all she gets,' snarled Billy.

'Prim?' repeated Mum.

'I'll have to think about it,' she said.

The next morning Prim got up very early, but not early enough for Big Bella. To her horror she saw her striding past the trailer window with a zombie-like look of aggression in her eyes. Without explanation, without breakfast and without waiting for her brothers, Prim dashed off and followed Big Bella at a distance. She's going to smash Patsy, thought Prim. And then there'll be more trouble and we'll get another reputation – this time for violence.

It was not long before they reached the school gates, outside which Big Bella positioned herself, stolid, hulk-like and threatening. Taking care to keep on the other side of the street and partly screened by the traffic, Prim managed to get past her without being spotted. Then she hurried on towards the motorway which rose up on stilts a few hundred yards away. But she didn't have to go as far as that – Patsy O'Bryan was sauntering towards her and she was on her own. With a sigh of relief, Prim went into action.

'Patsy.'

She came up to her suspiciously. 'How do you know my name?'

'Someone told me.'

'You still want trouble?'

'No, I've come to warn you. Someone else does.'

'Who?' she asked contemptuously.

'Big Bella.'

'Her? She's a thick twit.'

'She's a tough one.'

'I can handle her.'

'You sure?'

'Sure I'm sure. Now get out of my way.'

'We got our windows broke last night.'

'No concern of mine.'

'That's why Bella's after you.'

'So?'

'She's waiting by the gate. Waiting for you.'

'I told you – I can handle her.'

She pushed past Prim and walked on. Big Bella spotted her and stood, arms akimbo, blocking the school gates. She looked like a mountain. A mountain with fists. But Patsy simply walked on.

Prim closed her eyes. This was going to be very nasty indeed.

She could hear the blows. They were short, sharp and like sledge hammers. Then Big Bella turned away and walked back into the school. She was smiling with satisfaction. Prim ran up to Patsy who was staggering to her feet. Her nose and mouth were bleeding.

'I warned you,' said Prim.

'Leave me alone.' Tears ran down Patsy's cheeks.

'You'd better not tell any more fortunes.'

'I s'pose *you* put her up to it,' Patsy said.

'No,' said Prim. 'It was bound to happen – sooner or later. Look, can't we be friends?'

'Friends? With a pykie?'

'Friends. With a tinker?' Prim retorted.

'You want trouble?'

'You're in no state to give it. Why don't you let me mop you up?'

'I can look after myself,' Patsy insisted fiercely.

'Maybe. But you'll only be in trouble with the teachers. They'll say you've been fighting.'

'Fighting? I walked into a brick wall.'

'That's a good description of Bella.' Prim grinned at Patsy and drew first an unwilling smile, then, suddenly, surprisingly, a much more friendly grin.

'I s'pose it must have happened before,' said Patsy.

'What?'

'A tinker and a pykie getting together.'

'Maybe that's what the city does for us,' replied Prim, almost to herself. Then she said to Patsy, 'Come on – I'll help you get washed up.'

'Don't mind if you do,' said Patsy. But she grinned again.

38

## 3    *Blackie*

'There's going to be a trotting race, Vi,' said Reuben.

'Here?' Mum looked around her. 'They're going to close off the roads?'

'It's in the park – part of the carnival.'

Vi sniffed. 'Who's organised it – them social workers?'

'Carnival Committee.'

'Bound to be social workers on it.'

'Some of them are all right.'

'Yeah. Some.'

'So we're going in for it.'

'Only one small thing.'

'Now don't you go putting up your objections, Vi. We want to have a bit of fun. We *need* a bit of fun. Stuck on the streets like this.'

'It's only a small objection.'

'Well?' he asked abruptly.

'We haven't got a horse – or a cart.'

'Uncle Fred's got a cart he doesn't use. I can fetch it up from Orpington on the truck.'

'And the horse?'

'Thought we'd buy young Billy one.'

'Why Billy?'

'He's the eldest. They'll all have one in time.'

Vi considered. They'd got the money, for despite the difficulties of cutting up the scrap, they'd done well. And Billy had been a good boy. In fact in contrast with Len he was a saint. But you couldn't really contrast anyone with Len.

'All right then. Where you going to get the grie?'

'Down at Passion Joe's.'

'Gawd. Him?'

'Where else?'

'Watch you don't get done.'

'Have I ever been done?' Reuben was indignant.

'More times than I've had hot dinners,' Vi pronounced gloomily. 'And where you going to keep the grie then?' But Reuben was already bounding down the steps of the trailer.


'It's good out here.'

'Great.'

It was a beautiful Saturday morning, and Billy and his dad were driving out to Kent in the battered old truck.

'Are we going to buy a horse today, Dad?'

'You bet we are – I've got over eight hundred quid in twenties and fifties in me wallet.'

'Where're we going to keep it then?'

'I'll pay Passion Joe to keep it in his field – until we get out in the country again. And that won't be long. I'll bring you out here to ride him.'

'What about the trotting race?'

'Joe's got a horse box. He'll bring it up for me.'

'Dad—' Billy, normally willing to have a go at anything, was hesitant.

'Yeah?'

'I can't ride a horse.'

'You did when you was a kid.'

'I forgot.'

'You'll remember.'

'Can you ride a horse, Dad?'

'Sure. We was brought up on horses. You know that from your grandad.'

'What did Mum think about it all?'

'She had her objections – but she agreed in the end.'

'Good old Mum.'

They drove on in silence for a while as a light rain pattered down on the dusty heat-baked streets.

'Billy, how you getting on with your reading?'

'All right.'

'What's all right?'

'Not bad.'

'Your reading's important, boy. I can't read nor write – nor my father before me. And his father – and his father. I can't even fill in a form.'

'I could teach you, Dad,' said Billy eagerly.

'No,' said Reuben hastily. 'Too late for all that. But I want you to be a scholar – to really work at it.'

'Prim and Len are learning too.'

'But you're the eldest,' said Reuben in a holy sort

of voice. 'You're my eldest son. That's why you're having the horse first.'

Reuben drove the truck up a bumpy lane until they came to a huge field in which about twenty horses were grazing. There was a boy in the field. He was in his late teens and was riding one of the horses bareback. The field sloped up to a rise and on the top of it was a burnt-out trailer. Reuben froze.

'What's the matter, Dad?'

'I don't like the look of that,' he muttered. 'I don't like the look of that at all.'

'Of what? That trailer? What do you mean, Dad?'

But Reuben didn't answer. Instead he shouted across to the boy, 'Bubbles – Bubbles – come over here.'

Slowly the boy rode his horse over.

'What's going on then?' Reuben pointed at the charred shell of the trailer.

'It was his funeral.'

'You burnt him in the trailer?'

'That's what he would have wanted. It's the old ways.'

'Why wasn't I told?'

'Couldn't find you. The Penfolds said you were up London way. The Smiths said you'd gone to Surrey.'

'The Smiths always get it wrong. Trust them. Did he die peaceful?'

'Yes. He came wandering out here one evening – and he keeled right over amongst his horses.'

'Who's dead?' asked Billy.

'Passion Joe. He was an old man.'

'Eighty-nine,' said Bubbles proudly.

'His time was due. He was burnt in his trailer like he wanted.'

'Do the council allow it?' said Billy.

'To hell with the council. We've come about a horse.'

'Got the ready?'

'Plenty of it.'

'Who's it for?' asked Bubbles.

'It's for my boy. My eldest son. Billy boy here. I can buy it, but I'll have to leave it here. Till we get back to the country.'

'It'll cost you.'

'I can pay. So what happens then?'

'Grandad left them to me – what with Dad running off and all. I'll keep breeding. Horses that is.' He grinned. 'For the moment.'

'Do you sell 'em all?' asked Billy.

'Only to our own people.'

'Not to Gorgios?'

'Never.'

'Why not?'

'We never have. And it's not often I sell a horse to a chavvie. Not these days.'

'I want my kids to be brought up with 'em. It'll be better when we get back to the country.'

Billy winced. Dad must say this dozens of times every day, but he didn't manage to find anywhere.

And he hated the London site as much as they all did.

'Any sites?' asked Bubbles.

'Nothing,' said Reuben with a fierce sadness. 'Nothing at all.'

'Somewhere'll come up.'

'Yeah, it'll come up soon, won't it, Billy?'

'That's right, Dad.'

'Want to take a look round?' Bubbles proudly surveyed his horses.

'Come and see which one you'd like,' said Dad.

It was quite difficult at first and Billy was spoilt for choice. But suddenly it was obvious.

'That Blackie,' he said decisively.

'Where? Oh him – he's no good,' said Bubbles briskly.

'Why not?'

'He's stubborn – and slow.'

'Let me try him.'

'You don't want a slow one, son,' said Reuben. 'We wouldn't be able to race him.'

'Let me try him,' replied Billy firmly.

'He's broke in,' said Bubbles. 'He'll take a saddle.'

'Can I try him bareback?'

'If you want. But I can't be responsible—'

'You haven't ridden bareback since you were a kid,' chimed in Reuben. 'You should be careful.'

'And I've never ridden with a saddle. That's what I meant when I said I couldn't ride. I can ride bareback.'

Billy knew that his father and Bubbles were looking

at each other quizzically. Then Bubbles said: 'Give it a swing. It's soft ground to fall on. And he looks an athletic sort of kid.'

'He *is* an athletic sort of kid,' said Reuben with uneasy pride.

'Come on, boy.'

Blackie stood in the centre of the field staring at him.

'Come on.'

Billy felt that all the other horses were staring at him too – and Dad and Bubbles as well. But he was determined to succeed with Blackie. He didn't know what it was about him, but he had been immediately attracted to him. The question was – did Blackie feel the same?

'Come here, boy.'

But Blackie simply stood where he was, eyeing him steadily. He was jet black with rather a shaggy coat and a handsome white blaze between his eyes.

'Blackie.'

'It's not his name,' shouted Bubbles. 'I should have told you – it's Prince.'

'It's Blackie now,' said Billy stolidly. But then he whispered, 'Prince?' But still the horse didn't move. 'There,' he said. 'He doesn't know his name. Prince?' The horse was motionless. 'See what I mean?'

'Get on with it,' snapped Bubbles.

'Softly, softly,' muttered Billy. Quickly he grabbed Blackie's mane, slipped the bridle over his head and hauled himself up on the horse's back.

'You're my Blackie now,' he whispered.

Billy dug his heels in – and slowly Blackie broke into a shambling walk. He dug his heels in again and he reluctantly began to trot. He dug his heels in for the third time – and Blackie came to a dead stop, so abruptly that Billy was almost flung over his head and only hung on by gripping the horse with his knees.

'That's not bad,' said Bubbles.

'Not bad,' repeated Reuben, fingering his wallet.

On the way back Billy's behind was so sore that he kept wriggling on the hard front seat of the van. But he'd ridden Blackie for almost an hour, and although the horse had been stubborn and difficult, Billy still wanted him. So Dad bought him – and Billy was elated.

'You'll have to learn to ride with a saddle, boy.'

'OK, Dad.'

'You can't always ride bareback.'

'No, Dad.'

'Not nowadays you can't. He'll have to get used to being driven if you're going to enter him for trotting races.' Dad laughed. 'Not that he'll have a chance in hell in this one. In fact it's hardly worth—'

'He's going in it.'

'Well—'

'Can you run me – no – can I take some days off school – and stay with Bubbles and—'

'No.'

'Please, Dad.'

'Your Mum'd skin me alive, boy.'

'Dad – if I could – if I *could* stay with Bubbles I'd get Blackie to win.'

'No way.'

'If I rode him bareback.'

'Saddle or nothing. Think it out, boy. You'll need the cart too.'

'Bubbles could teach me. I'll get Blackie to win. Honest, Dad.'

Reuben paused and looked at Billy for a moment. When his gaze returned to the road he had another thought. Billy was growing up. In a few years he'd be a man. His boy. All right – maybe he *should* let him. Maybe learning to ride Blackie was part of his growing up. But what Vi would say he dreaded to think.

'All right.'

'You mean I can go?'

'Next weekend – Saturday, Sunday, Monday. I'll phone Bubbles – I got his number. That way you'll only miss one day of school. So you'll have to work fast.'

'Thanks, Dad.'

'And that's my final word.'

'I'll do it, Dad – I'll get Blackie to win.'

'Look—'

'I will. You *have* to get that cart.'

'OK.'

'And, Dad—'

47

'Yes?' Suddenly Reuben felt tired. He'd have to go down the pub for a quick one before he faced Vi.

'Are they taking bets on this race?'

'They would be. But there's no point in—'

'Blackie *will* win.'

'OK – but I'm not losing money.'

'All right.'

'Eh?'

'I said all right.'

Reuben was puzzled. It wasn't like Billy boy to give in so quickly, so meekly. Suddenly Reuben smelt trouble.

'Billy?'

'Yes, Dad?'

'What are you up to?'

'Nothing.'


Billy was sitting in the park after school on Monday with Toey – his best friend from the site. There was no one else around and the clouds above them were bulging with rain.

'You in the race?' asked Billy.

'No – but I'm taking some bets.'

'You are, are you? What about placing some on me?'

'You are an outsider, mate – rank outsider.'

'Who's the favourite?'

'Charlie Smith.'

'Oh him. Are Gorgios in this?'

'No. Romany event. We don't want no one else.'

'Can I put a bet on myself?'

'You'd be a fool if you did.'

'But I'm going to win – me and Blackie.'

'This the horse your dad bought you?' asked Toey cautiously.

'Yeah.'

'Driven it at all?'

'It's down at Passion Joe's. Bubbles has taken over since the old man died. I'm going down there for the weekend.'

'And then?'

'I'll win. I'll work at it. So can I place that bet?'

'Billy, you mustn't do this. Your mum and dad would go mad.'

'Mum already has – 'bout me missing a day's school while I'm at Bubbles'. She's not speaking to Dad.'

'There you are then.'

'But she'll be in a good mood when I win five hundred quid.'

'Five hundred? You're barmy.'

'How much do I have to bet to win five hundred?'

'The odds on you are ten to one so it would be fifty,' Toey told him. Then he said, 'You shouldn't do this, Billy.'

'Why not?'

'It's too soon – you're throwing it away.'

'You refusing to take my bet?'

'No. I'm just warning you, that's all. What happens if you lose?'

'I won't,' said Billy. 'I'm confident, I am.'

*

Ten days later, the park was covered in bunting and the horses and carts gleamed with grooming and polish. Perched in the driving seat, Billy pulled at Blackie's reins gently. He felt that the three days with Bubbles had gone well, and even Bubbles had grudgingly admitted that he had done 'all right'. At night Billy had slept exhausted in Bubbles' trailer, and all day he had spent in the field with Blackie, first of all riding bareback and then learning to use saddle and finally the long driving reins. Gradually the horse had become more obedient, and each time they learnt something together Billy loved Blackie just that little bit more. He had even grown used to his new name – Billy was sure of that. So he felt supremely confident as he waited with eight other carts for the start of the race. He was not only confident but proud, as he saw his family standing there: Mum and Dad, Prim and Len and his grandparents up here for the special occasion. Even the sight of the gloomy-looking Toey did not deter him, not even when Toey said:

'It's not too late to cancel that bet, Billy.'

'Don't need to – I'm going to win.'

'You're a right stinger and no mistake.'

'Get lost!'

'Your mum'll—'

'Get lost!'

Toey shrugged and walked away. Then Vi came across. 'What's all that about?'

'Nothing, Mum.'

'There's something going on.'

'Quick – they're starting.'

She backed away, the crowd went silent and for the first time Billy felt a tremor of nerves.

'On your marks – get set – go.'

'Come on, Blackie,' whispered Billy.

All the horses began to trot, there was a roar from the crowd, they trotted faster – and Blackie remained absolutely still.

'Come on! Come on, Blackie!' said Billy desperately.

But he remained utterly motionless, except for a disdainful flick of his tail.

Then a Traveller in the crowd shouted: 'Isn't that Prince? One of poor old Passion Joe's nags? Prince. Prince. Giddy up there.'

And Blackie moved slowly forward. Then he began to trot – but far too late.

Billy glanced across at the crowd. He felt hot and cold at the same time. He saw that Toey was talking to Mum. He'd fix him for that. Then he felt a roaring in his ears as Blackie trotted sedately on, well behind the others. He looked in front of him and imagined a big, black pit. If only it would open up and swallow him.

# 4    *Fruiting*


'Billy!'

No reply.

'Billy!'

'Yes, Mum.' His voice was sullen. He had kept away from them all after the trotting race. Not only had it been the most dreadful humiliation, but he was desperately ashamed that Dad had had to pay fifty quid to Toey. And Mum had been really furious with him.

'Got some good news for you. For us all.' She sounded different, totally different, much more like the old Mum he used to know.

'What's up?'

'We got a site – a site in the country.'

'Whereabouts, Mum?'

'Appledore – near the Marsh. In an old orchard.'

'How did Dad get that?'

'He heard about it at the carnival. The farm's gone bust but the old lady who owns it isn't selling up. She wants to stay put, so she's going to raise a crop of trailers instead.'

'Romanies?'

'All of us.'

'Great. Mum – can we – can we get Blackie across?'

Mum frowned. 'After all the trouble that horse has caused us – what with your dad losing all that money—'

'Please, Mum—'

'And you being that cocksure! I've never felt such a fool in me life. And making bets with that Toey!'

'Mum!'

'All right then. But you're looking after that nag yourself. All the time.'

Billy got off his bunk and flung his arms round his mother's neck.

'You always get round me,' she said in a muffled voice.


'Is it safe, Dad?' Prim was wrapping up all the china in the posh trailer, ready for the move to Appledore.

'Safe?'

'I mean – can we stay there forever?'

'The old girl says we can – and I'm paying her a fair rent.'

'What's it like?'

'Bit tumbledown. But we'll soon have it straight.'

'And Grandma – and Grandad – they'll be coming?'

'They'll bring their trailer.'

'What about the others?'

'There's the Jordans and the Bignells, the Penfolds and the Smiths. Not too big – good size.'

Prim nodded. It sounded wonderful. All the families got on well together. But what was the catch? For they had done so much moving about that there must be a catch. Somewhere.

'Billy.'

'What's up, Len?'

For once Len seemed subdued as Billy cleaned up the old truck that, with Mum's van, would tow them back to the country.

'Do you want to go?'

'Yeah. I'll have Blackie.'

'I'll miss me mates.'

'That lot?'

'They're me mates.'

'We've only been here a couple of months.'

'But I got me mates,' said Len pathetically.

'You'll get new ones – we're going to a new school.'

Len sniffed and kicked at a can on the ground. 'It's all right for you.'

'Why?'

'You got your horse.'

'You'll be all right, Len,' said Billy, looking at him affectionately. He was a tough little scruff most of the time, but he had his moments when you could feel sorry for him.

'I don't fancy the country.'

'Why not?'

'It's spooky at night. There's lights up here.'

'Blimey, Len, you've been brought up in the country.'

54

'Yeah, and I don't want to go back. I've got me mates – and they're not all Romanies neither.'

'Don't you want your own people?'

'I know other ones now. All kinds of people.'

'Why don't you do something useful? Like clean Mum's van for a start.' Billy was fast losing sympathy.

'You can stick that.'

Billy leapt over to belt him but missed. Len laughed mockingly and repeated, 'You can stick that.'

'I heard you the first time, Len. Now get lost!'

'I bet it's a dump.'

'Shut up!'

'I bet it's a dump we're going to.'

In fact the old orchard lived up to Len's expectations. It was covered in rusting farm machinery, wooden boxes, an old car and the skeleton of a truck.

'We'll soon get it right,' said Reuben stolidly.

Vi groaned. 'We *would* be the first mugs to move in.'

'Told you it'd be a dump,' said Len triumphantly.

They all turned on him this time, but before Len could receive the full blast of the Roberts' anger, Reuben said hastily, 'Here comes Mrs Pringle. She's a bit . . . a bit . . . odd.'

Vi raised her eyebrows. 'Anything else you got to tell us about this place?'

He shook his head. 'She's the lot,' he said.

She certainly was. Mrs Pringle was wearing an old

55

over-sized mac that trailed on the ground behind her and a large straw hat. She had long white hair and her face was covered in powder. Her lips were a bright red lipstick gash, but she was upright and had a certain wild dignity as she trampled over the long grass towards them.

'Mrs Pringle.' Reuben went up to her with an outstretched hand. 'How are you?'

'Who are you?' she asked crossly.

It took Reuben some minutes of urgent explanation to establish who they were and what she had promised. Vi stood with her arms folded, and Reuben felt as desperate as Billy had when Blackie had refused to start in the trotting race. Then came the break through.

'Oh, I remember. You're Mr Roberts.'

'That's correct, madam.'

'You're coming to live here. In my orchard.'

'I'm paying you rent, madam.'

'Are you?' she asked vaguely.

'And so are the others.'

'The others?'

'The Jordans, the Bignells, the Penfolds and the Smiths. They're all coming here.'

'Are they?'

'Yes. That was our agreement.'

'Well, that will be nice. It's been a bit lonely since I had to sell the dairy herd and get rid of my manager. It wasn't paying, you see.'

'No, madam.'

Prim thought that her dad sounded like a butler on the telly, he was so respectful to the old lady. But she knew her mum was furious. Was Mrs Pringle capable of remembering anything?

'You're a Romany, aren't you? Mr . . . Mr . . .'

'Roberts,' said Vi bleakly.

'Mr Roberts.'

'That's right, madam.'

She looked around the orchard as if seeing it for the first time. 'This used to be one of the loveliest orchards in Kent.'

'Was it?' asked Vi wearily.

'I used to love the Travellers coming. Fruiting, they called it. The whole orchard would be lit up with oil lamps and cooking fires, children scampering about the trees, old Rosie singing. Of course, she still does . . .' Mrs Pringle's voice died away. 'When my husband was alive, he used to say, "I can still hear her, Megan." Well – I couldn't then, but I can now. Dear old Rosie.'

'You mean – she's around still?' asked Len with sudden suspicion.

'Around? She's been dead twenty years.'

'But you said – you said she was still singing.'

'Oh yes,' said Mrs Pringle, the vague look wafting back into her eyes. 'She still sings.'

'She's a ghost then.' Len turned on Billy accusingly. 'See what I mean? I told you it was going to be spooky.'

Vi cleared her throat impatiently. 'Mrs Pringle – my husband had a contract drawn up between us.'

'Did he?'

'Can I see it?'

'Yes, there is a bit of paper. It's in the house somewhere. I'll bring it out presently.'

'Thank you.' Vi turned accusingly to Reuben and hissed, 'I don't like all this.'

'It'll be fine,' he said, looking round at the overgrown hawthorn hedges, the broken apple trees and the wreckage. 'Once we get this lot cleared.'

The Roberts spent the rest of the day moving old machinery, shifting piles of wood and then towing the trailer into the orchard. Bubbles was bringing Blackie down that evening and, despite everything, Billy was feeling happy. The orchard smelt good – of apples and bonfires and sweet scented earth. It was a smell he had got used to when he was a child – the smell of freedom. Even Len seemed to cheer up during the clearing and Mum actually broke into song. The other families were not due to arrive for a couple of days and Reuben winked at Billy as they hauled an old ploughshare out of the orchard.

'It's going to be all right,' he said. 'Your mum likes it here.'

Later Billy asked Prim what she felt.

'It's good,' she said, 'smells good.'

The September night was soft and warm and Reuben lit a fire and Vi made a fry-up. It was delicious eating it in the open air.

At about nine Bubbles brought Blackie, who at first refused to come into the orchard at all.

'Typical of that horse,' said Vi. 'Absolutely typical.'

But eventually Blackie was persuaded to come in, and after a while he seemed to roam round the old apple trees quite happily.

Vi then made Bubbles something to eat and they all sat round the fire drinking hot, strong tea sweetened with condensed milk.

'We're back to the old life,' pronounced Reuben. 'And we'll never leave it again.'

'She really has agreed to let you cut up the motors here?' asked Prim.

'Yeah. We're going to use the old farmyard.' Reuben grinned at her across the flames of the campfire. 'You all right, Prim?'

She sipped her tea. 'Hope school'll be OK.'

'You bet it will,' said Vi. She seemed to be in increasing good spirits.

'I miss me mates,' began Len.

'You'll make some more,' she said comfortingly and drew him into her arms. After a few minutes of being snuggled up to her, Len was asleep.

'You'll have to be careful,' said Bubbles to Reuben before he left.

'What about?'

'Has she got council permission?'

'Eh?'

'Change of use? Trailers in the orchard. Cutting up motors in the farmyard.'

'Dunno. Does she need it? It's none of their business.'

'The council? It is. They might not grant it.'

'Reckon we'd better keep quiet. She's pretty barmy.'

'So she hasn't got it?'

Reuben opened the gate, looking back to make sure Vi was not listening to the conversation. He sighed with relief; he was sure that she was out of earshot.

'Don't let Vi know about this. She'll go spare.'

'OK – but what you going to do?'

'Nothing,' said Reuben firmly.

'Time you was in bed, son.'

'Let me stay a bit longer, Mum,' said Billy as he stroked Blackie's forehead. 'I've got to give him a brush before I go to bed.'

'Make it snappy – and you, Prim.'

'OK, Mum.'

Vi stood up stiffly, still clasping Len to her. 'I'd better put this mite to bed.'

She went back to the trailer, and Len's face, lying on her shoulder, looked unnaturally angelic.

Prim and Billy didn't say anything to each other – they just wanted to savour the magic of the night air. They both knew that it meant a great deal to them, and the weeks spent in London just seemed like a dusty memory.

Then Prim said quietly: 'What's that?'

'What's what?'

'Listen—'

Suddenly Blackie shivered.

'I can't hear—'

'Listen!'

Then he heard it and Blackie shivered again. It was very soft, almost indistinct. Then it grew just a fraction louder. Someone was singing down at the bottom of the orchard.

*'The old ways are changing, you cannot deny*
*The day of the traveller's over.*
*There's nowhere to go and there's nowhere to bide,*
*So farewell to the life of the rover.'*

'Blimey,' hissed Billy. 'It's the ghost of old Rosie. She's out there – down the bottom. Look at Blackie.'

The horse was rigid, its head up. A slight breeze stirred the apple trees and they whispered softly and gently as the song continued.

'If Len hears that – he'll go bananas,' breathed Prim.

'He's flat out,' muttered Billy. The words had died away but they still seemed to hang in the air above them in the velvet night.

'Well, I don't believe in ghosts,' said Prim.

'I do,' replied Billy. Blackie was relaxing now but he still kept sniffing the air.

'So I'm going to take a look.'

'What?'

'Take a look down the bottom of the orchard.'

61

'You're barmy.'

'You coming?'

'What?'

'I *said* – you coming?'

'I don't want to.' Billy paused indecisively.

'So you'll let *me* go alone?'

'No. No, I won't.'

'Come on then.'

'Gawd! Suppose it really is a ghost?'

'Then we'll see one for the first time.'

'Maybe it's gone – probably vanished.'

'Yeah? Listen.'

At first the words were so soft that they were like part of the breeze. Then they could just make them out again.

Billy grabbed protectively at Blackie's mane. The voice was quiet, quavery, yet it carried so clearly.

'I don't want to leave Blackie.'

'Bring him then.'

'Come on, Blackie.' At first Billy thought that the horse would be stubborn again and stay rooted to the spot. Then he began to move – far too fast for Billy's liking – down to the bottom of the orchard.

They had covered about fifty yards when Prim said, 'Hang on.'

'What's up?'

'I thought I saw something move.'

'Gawd!'

'Come *on*.'

'Not if something – somebody's moving.'

'They're not now.'

Billy reluctantly started to walk again with Blackie happily following. Then they both saw the figure. At the bottom of the orchard was a kind of broken-down summer-house. And in it, someone was sitting, no longer singing but staring out over a tangled thicket of what might once have been a flower-bed.

'Who's there?' asked Prim in a thread of a voice.

'It's me.'

'Who?'

'It's me – Mrs Pringle. Who's that?'

Billy felt swooping, soaring relief. It was fantastic – only Mrs Pringle and not a ghost after all. He felt like leaping for joy.

'Prim and Billy Roberts.'

'The Romanies? How lovely.' She stood up. She was dressed in a long skirt with about three cardigans over it, topped by an immense shawl.

'You were singing – we thought you were old Rosie.'

'Old who?'

'The ghost. Old Rosie.'

'She's dead. Rosie's dead.' She paused. 'She taught me that song. Did I frighten you with it?'

'No,' said Billy, not looking at Prim and stroking Blackie's mane. 'You didn't frighten us at all.'

'I often come and sit here – used to be our favourite place . . . me and my husband's. I can't sleep now, you see.'

'You ought to come and sit round our camp-fire if you can't sleep,' said Billy.

'I'd like that.'

'Come on,' said Prim. 'Let me see you back to the house.' She took Mrs Pringle's arm and helped her up.

'I hope I didn't frighten you,' she said again as Prim guided her over the rough grass.

Prim smiled. 'If Billy says you didn't – you didn't.'

'He's a brave lad, is he?' muttered Mrs Pringle.

'Very brave,' said Prim, smiling.

Billy looked quickly away.

# 5    *The Burning*

'How long have you been here?' she asked.

'Couple of weeks.' Reuben poked at the dead ashes in the fire while Vi brought out tea from the trailer.

'And the kids? They're in school?'

'Little local place. They like it – even Len. And Billy's got his horse.'

'Can you stay here?'

Reuben looked round at the other trailers that had been brought into the orchard. Some women were moving about inside them; the men were out in the farmyard, cutting up scrap with acetylene torches.

'We're staying. No one's moving us on this time.'

'I'm sorry about Solly,' said Vi.

'He was old – as old as Passion Joe. And that's the way he would have wanted his funeral too.' Leah Bell was Solly's daughter. She was a big, comfortable, middle-aged woman. But now there was a firmness to her mouth and a look of steel in her eyes. 'They didn't want to know,' she said slowly.

'What's wrong then? Can't you burn him?'

'In the vardo? That council? They said definitely no.'

'Passion Joe got away with it.'

'Yeah. But Solly hasn't.'

'Where is he?'

'Still in the vardo. In his coffin. All dressed up – and nowhere to go.'

'You can't keep him there,' said Reuben.

'Well, I just don't know what to do. He wouldn't want to go in the ground. That was his last wish – to be burnt in his vardo.'

'We could ask Mrs Pringle,' said Vi hesitantly. 'She's a bit odd, but we know she's fond of our kind. I mean – there was old Rosie. I wonder if she was buried?'

'You mean – bring him all the way down here?'

'Why not? If she agrees.'

'That vardo's really old; I don't think it would make the journey.'

'I'll get someone to bring it down on a truck,' said Reuben. 'Tie it on secure – it'll be OK.'

'Well . . .'

'Give it a swing, Leah,' urged Vi.

'It's very good of you of course . . .'

'Where else could you do it then?' challenged Reuben. 'Our people need to keep up the traditions – or they'll all go.'

Leah shook her head. 'I didn't know *what* to do,' she repeated.

'Mrs Pringle was singing a sad song the other night, about the old ways going – learnt it off old Rosie.'

66

'I remember her at the fruiting.'

'Yeah. The kids thought it *was* old Rosie singing – had the fright of their lives. But Mrs Pringle it was all the time – and she sang it again for me the next morning. She must have had a nice voice once.'

'But don't you see – all the old ways *are* going,' said Reuben. 'We've got a duty to keep 'em up, *and* fetch 'em back if necessary.'

'Solly would be pleased with this talk.' Leah was visibly moved and a tear ran down her brown cheek.

'We'll give him a good send off,' said Reuben. 'It'll be real style.'

'Want to come in with me, Prim?' asked Vi uneasily.

'OK, Mum.'

'Truth is, I don't like going into houses as you know. And particularly hers.'

'Why particularly hers?' Prim's voice was flat. She'd had a bad day at school. Although she'd told her parents she was enjoying life at the village school, she was actually finding it very difficult. There were only a few Travellers' children, and they all came from Mrs Pringle's orchard. They tended to stick together, and although the other children in the school weren't unkind, they left them as a group. Prim wanted a Gorgio friend, but stood little chance of getting one, and she was fed up with hanging around with the other Travellers, especially as Len kept going on about his London mates all the time.

'Because it'll be funny,' said Mum. 'Very funny.'

\*

It was. But Mrs Pringle's home was also very sad; she had obviously just let it go to pieces. Once it had been very posh, with beautifully-furnished rooms, but now the tables were covered with dishes of uneaten food, dirty plates and old newspapers. The newspapers were piled up on the floor too, and at least half a dozen cats were prowling about.

'Mrs Pringle?' Vi called.

But there was no reply.

'Mrs Pringle?'

Still no reply.

'We'll have to look for her.'

Eventually they found her in a very small room just by the stairs. It had obviously once been a study, and she was sitting at a dusty table, leafing over the pages of a photograph album.

'Are you from the village?' she asked.

'It's Mrs Roberts, dear, and Primrose.'

'You want jumble?'

'No, love. We're in your orchard.'

'Apple picking?'

'We live there. We're your Romanies,' said Vi in a very measured voice.

'Of course you are. Why didn't you say so earlier?' She looked up from the album on which she was using a magnifying glass. 'Can I help you?'

'I want to ask you a favour.'

'Ask away.'

'Well – er – you know your song – the song Rosie taught you?' Vi gave her a couple of lines:

68

*'Farewell to the cant and the travelling tongue*
*Farewell to the Romany talking—'*
Amazingly, Mrs Pringle remembered. 'Oh yes, dear—
*The buying and selling, the old fortune telling*
*The knock on the door and the hawking,'*
she finished tremulously.

'That's it. Well, we don't want these old Romany customs to die out, do we?'

'Certainly not.'

'Of course – one old custom is rather sad, but . . . well . . . it's important to us. When a Romany dies – they're usually burnt in their caravans.'

'Are they?'

Vi's heart sank; that was obviously something that old Rosie didn't pass on.

'It's like cremation,' said Prim, trying to strike a chord.

'Oh yes.'

'Well, old Solly Bell's gone and snuffed it – I mean – tragically died. Of course he was pretty old. Now his daughter Leah – she can't get the council to allow a caravan burning.'

'Do I know these people?' asked Mrs Pringle vaguely.

'Er, no. But we do.'

'Yes. How can I help?' Her eyes were misty.

'Well . . . I wondered . . . if we got the caravan brought down here, could we burn it in one of your fields?'

'With Mr Solly in it?'

'With Mr Bell in it.'

'And he's dead—?'

'So he won't come to any harm,' said Prim and giggled.

Vi gave her a nasty look, but Mrs Pringle only nodded and said, 'Yes. I realise he's dead. Thank you. Well, Mrs Appleyard—'

'Mrs Roberts,' corrected Vi.

'I'm sure that will be quite in order.'

'You mean you don't mind?'

'Not at all. I'm very anxious to keep these old traditions going for the Red Cross—'

'For the Romanies,' put in Prim, knowing that she was going to burst out laughing any moment.

'For the Romanies,' agreed Mrs Pringle, returning to her magnifying glass and photograph album. 'So pleased. Good-day.'

'Cor – he's going to be in it when they burn it?' Len hopped around in excited anticipation.

'Well, he's not going to be on the roof,' said Mum as she knitted on the trailer steps. She smiled at Prim. 'You know that little bit of grass I used to look at up in Deptford, now I can really look at it all. And since your dad and the others have shifted all the junk – why it's like paradise.'

'I'm pleased for you, Mum.'

'You all right, Prim?'

'Course I am.'

'You just don't seem your normal happy-go-lucky self.'

70

'I'm fine, Mum. Honest.'

'Can we see him *before* they burn it?' asked Len.

Prim was grateful for the intervention as she and Mum turned on Len in their usual way. 'Shut up, you!' they chorused.

But Len was not entirely insensitive. 'You know why Prim ain't normal?'

'Thanks,' she snapped.

'It's because she's got to go around with us lot all the time.'

'What do you mean by that?' asked Vi sharply.

'Shut up, Len.'

'We have to stick together – us Travellers. They don't want to know us – the other kids – that's why I miss me mates in London.'

'Is this true, Prim?'

'No.'

'It *is*, Mum. She just won't admit it.'

'You mean – they – they – won't speak to you?'

'Don't listen to him, Mum. He's exaggerating everything – as usual.'

Len stuck his tongue out at his sister. Just then, Billy came up with Blackie.

'Billy.'

'Yes, Mum?'

'This true about school – about the other kids not speaking to you?'

'It's not as bad as that.'

'Well, what is it as bad as?'

'There're just a few of us – and an awful lot of them.'

'Don't they play with you?'

'Not a lot.'

'I'm going in to that teacher then.'

'Don't do that, Mum. You'll make it worse,' protested Billy.

'I'm not having it.'

'Leave it, Mum,' said Prim quietly. 'We'll sort it out. Won't we, Billy?'

Billy nodded. 'You bet.'

'It *was* better in London,' Len informed them.


Between them, Leah and Reuben organised matters very quickly, and a day later the vardo arrived on top of a large truck. Behind the truck came a procession of cars and vans and other trucks. Reuben let them all into Mrs Pringle's top field which grew long grass rather than any kind of crop. Despite the closure of the farm she had, so far, failed to sell any of the land.

'Where is he?' asked Len.

'Who?' Leah looked at him, puzzled.

'Solly.'

'He's in that van.'

'In his coffin?'

'That's right.'

'Let's have a squint.'

'You'll see it in a minute. We're going to put it in the vardo once we've off-loaded it.'

'Go on, missus. Let's have a look.'

'Oh, all right.' Leah grinned at him. 'Right little morbid tyke, aren't you?' She opened the back doors of the van. On the floor was a beautifully varnished coffin, covered in wreaths. 'That's Solly.'

'He's inside? Straight up?'

'Of course he's inside. Unless they got the bodies mixed up at the undertakers.'

'Do you think they did?' asked Len. 'I mean, any old geezer could be in there.'

'Well, he's not. That's my dad.'

'You checked?'

'Yeah.'

'How did he look?'

'Peaceful.'

'You upset then?'

'I was – but he was an old 'un. Almost ninety. It was his time to go.'

'You still upset? You mourning?'

Leah ruffled Len's untidy hair. 'No,' she said. 'Talking to you cheers me up.'

'You mean it?'

'I mean it.' Leah bent down and kissed him on his grubby cheek.

The ceremony was very moving. The coffin was carried shoulder-high by four sturdy Travellers, and then placed gently, reverently, in one of the most gorgeous painted vardos that Billy had ever seen.

'It's what they call – the Gorgios call – a real gypsy caravan,' sniffed Vi.

'Anyone going to say any prayers?' asked Len.

'We'll whisper in the wind,' said Grandad. 'That's what we'll do, my boy.'

The Travellers – about two hundred of them – then formed a ring round the vardo. Then one of Solly's brothers – another old, gnarled man – said, 'We'll torch the vardo.' Billy and Prim felt salty tears on their cheeks and Len looked on in a kind of wonderment.

'Where was he born?' hissed Len at Leah.

'At Bell Street Green,' she said. 'In a vardo just like that.' She took Len's hand. 'Wish I'd got a man to see me through this – but he walked out on me. And all me kiddies scattered and gone.'

'You got me,' said Len hopefully. 'I'm a man.'

Billy was just about to say, 'You're a runt,' when he stopped himself and looked up at Mum who was smiling through her tears.

'You gotta say this for our Len,' she whispered to Billy and Prim. 'He turns up trumps. At the last minute the boy turns up trumps.'

They both had to agree.

A younger man went up the steps with a blazing torch made of sticks and he threw it inside the vardo. Someone else followed with another torch – and another and another. Smoke came from the door and soon the whole vardo was ablaze from end to end.

'Goodbye, Dad,' cried Leah.

Len clasped her hand tightly.

'Goodbye, Dad,' she repeated. Then she swept Len into her arms and began to sob.

Soon the vardo was reduced to a charred heap of

wood, and little vapour trails of smoke spiralled upwards in the September afternoon. There was a smell of woodsmoke and blackberries and Billy could see them plump and glistening in the hedgerow. The crowd of Travellers watched the glowing remains for a long time. Then Vi took Leah by the arm and said, 'Let's have a cuppa.'

This was the signal for everyone to start moving back to the orchard where Vi and some of the other women had erected a trestle table groaning with sandwiches and cakes. A big tea urn had been set up on the far end of the table and, strangely enough, Mrs Pringle was behind it, shakily dispensing slopped tea. 'It's so wonderful to have a fête again,' she was saying to an elderly Travelling man. 'Have you seen the vicar?' Later on she said to Reuben, 'And what about the tombola?'

'What about it?' Reuben asked before Vi hushed him.

A few minutes later, Len shouldered his way through the crowd to the sandwiches. 'Mum.'

'Don't bother me now, love. Can't you see I'm rushed off me feet?'

'I got to talk to you.'

'Not *now*.'

Then Billy arrived. 'Len's trying to tell you the police are here,' he said.

'Are you in charge here, sir?' asked the young police constable.

Reuben shifted uneasily. 'Well—'

'Only we've had a complaint.'

'About what?'

'I gather a caravan has been burnt in that field. Your neighbours weren't that pleased. Can you tell me how it came to be on fire?'

'It's a funeral,' said Vi.

'I take it—'

'Yes, we're Travellers.'

'And the funeral—'

'Solly Bell. It's a tradition. He was cremated in his vardo.'

'I see. And – was permission sought?'

'From who?'

'Er – the Local Authority.'

'It's nothing to do with them,' said Reuben belligerently. 'What's it got to do with them? This is a private occasion – and we're on private land.'

'This is Mrs Pringle's farm.'

'We have a lease. Do you want to speak to her?'

'Does she have permission for a change of use?'

'Course she does.'

But Vi could feel herself going cold. She knew this was the start of them moving on again. It had only been a matter of time.

Then Mrs Pringle wandered up. 'Welcome to the fête,' she said to the officer. 'Have you visited the tombola?'

# 6    *My Mother Said . . .*

A few days later Mrs Pringle showed Vi a letter from the Local Authority.

'It's no good, love. I can't read. Shall I get my Billy?'

'You can't read?' Everything came as a surprise to Mrs Pringle. 'What a shame. Didn't you go to school?'

'Just read it to me. Please.' Vi couldn't bear going through everything again with her. She had told her so many times.

'*Dear Madam,*

*I understand a change of use has occurred on your land in that a number of caravans have been parked in your orchard. This is in direct contravention of the Town & Country Planning Act, 1971 and I would ask you to ensure the caravans are removed within the next seven days.*

> *Yours faithfully,*
> *T J Butterworth*
> *Planning Officer.*'

'All right,' said Vi immediately. 'We'll go.'

'Go?'

'That's what the man wants.'

'You're not going to make a fight of it?' Quite suddenly Mrs Pringle was no longer vague.

'But—'

'I think you should.'

'It's your land, Mrs Pringle. I wouldn't like you to get into trouble.'

'Trouble? This is your *home*.'

'Yes, but . . . I mean—'

'So I think we *should* make a fight of it.'

'You could go to prison.'

'Now that *would* be interesting—'

'Mrs Pringle,' began Vi. 'I don't think you realise how—'

'Oh, but I *do* realise. I realise everything. You need a home. You keep being moved on. You mustn't be moved on from here.'

'Er—' Vi was amazed by Mrs Pringle's sudden acuteness. It was incredible. But maybe that was what she had needed. A fight. A cause.

'Now, Vi,' said Mrs Pringle briskly. 'I wonder if you'd bring your husband to tea this afternoon. Would he be available then?'

'Oh, yes.'

'I think we should make some plans.'

It was raining, and Prim, Billy, Len, Arnie, Cissie, Tommy and Abe were sitting in a classroom playing

78

cards. This was what they always did if it rained. If it was good weather they'd wander about in a group. They weren't asked to join in the other children's games, though if they asked to be included they usually were. But they always had to ask, and after a while they had got tired of doing so. One of the teachers had tried to get the two groups together, and for a while they dutifully tried, but they soon separated up again. Somehow, after a few weeks, the Travelling children had all, rather sadly, accustomed themselves to it – everyone except Prim, who was finding it more and more unbearable. She so longed to have a Gorgio friend, to know something of what it was like in the outside world. She had almost had one such friend in London, but then they had had to move back to the country. I don't stand a chance, thought Prim miserably. The Travelling community was the very centre of her world, and everything else radiated out from it, but she felt she was riveted at that centre, never seeing what lay beyond. So Prim was always searching for an opportunity, but never quite grasping it at the right time. Then, unexpectedly, something happened that gave her the chance she wanted.

Mrs Crimble, the Head Teacher, made an announcement at the end of assembly. 'And by the way, Susan Lake lost a five pound note on the playing field yesterday. If anyone finds it, please hand it in.'

It was this very simple announcement that gave Prim the idea. At first she rejected it – it was just too stupid. Also, why should she do it? Then Prim thought of Susan. She was a very popular girl – perhaps *the* most popular girl in the school. If she could get in with her, claim her friendship in one desperate act, then this could be the passport to other friendships with other girls. No longer would she be 'that gypsy girl – you know – she hangs around with them all the time', but instead, she would be 'that gypsy girl who's so popular with everyone'.

Once, when she had asked her about marriage, Mum had said, 'We'll find you a nice boy.'

Prim had resented that; it was like one of those Eastern marriages where everything was arranged and you had no choice. It really is as bad as that, she thought, amongst some of the Romanies. Summoning up her courage she had asked Mum, 'S'pose I want to marry a Gorgio?'

Mum had laughed. 'You won't be doing that.'

'Why not?'

'Because those that do have terrible lives.'

'But why should they?'

Mum had shaken her head. 'Marrying outside their own kind – that's what does it.'

'But some of us must marry outside – and be happy.'

Mum, however, was not to be drawn into being generous. 'I don't know a single one,' she had pronounced with gloomy relish.

Now, with that conversation in mind, Prim was

determined to take the greatest risk she had ever taken in her life.

'Susan?'

'Yes?' Did she look at her coldly, or was it just Prim's imagination.

'I found your fiver.'

'You what?'

'On the field. Look – it's a bit damp.'

'Pru—'

'The name's Prim.'

'Prim – you're great. My mum was going to flay me alive. It's money for a new blouse and – oh, Prim, thanks. Come and tell Mrs Crimble.'

They told her and she congratulated Prim. 'Now that was very honest of you, my dear.'

Would she have said that to a Gorgio, wondered Prim, stressing the honesty and all that, or was she just being over-sensitive. She was certainly being foolhardy for she could hardly believe the enormity of what she was doing. But she was desperate.

Sure enough, as she and Susan walked back into the playground, Susan said, 'I'm really grateful, you know.'

'That's all right.'

'I tell you what, Pru—'

'Prim.'

'Sorry, Prim. What's that short for?'

'Primrose.'

81

'Golly – that's unusual. Do all gypsies have funny names?'

Prim almost said – that's not a funny name. Then she changed her mind.

'We have different ones.'

'I tell you what – why don't you come home and have some tea? My mum would love to thank you.'

'When?'

'Tomorrow.'

'Great. And I'll tell *you* what.'

'Yes?'

'How about coming home with me?'

There was a fractional pause.

'Tonight.'

Another fractional pause. Then: 'My mum doesn't know—'

'Why don't you ring her?'

'*Ring* her?' She sounded as if the idea was unheard of. But Susan had not bargained for Prim's insistence. For Prim couldn't resist the immediate idea of, for once, bringing a Gorgio home. And the idea excited her so much that she wanted it now, now. And she wouldn't settle for anything else.

'You could come and see our trailer – I mean caravan – and my brother Billy's got a horse.' That clinched it, Prim could see with sudden elation. She'd caught her.

'I've always wanted a horse, but my parents won't let me.'

'You could ride Blackie,' Prim said, taking another

enormous risk. No one rode Blackie but Billy. She would have to bribe him somehow.

'Well . . .'

'You could ride him in the woods.'

'All right. I'll ring my mum. But I don't know if she'll agree. Who'll take me home?'

'Where do you live?'

'Leaves Close.'

'That's near. I'll walk back with you. And you can go when you like,' added Prim pathetically.

Then Susan said something very odd. She began to chant:

*'My mother said
I never should
Play with the gypsies in the wood.
If I did,
She would say,
Naughty girl to disobey.'*

She giggled and Prim went red. Susan didn't seem to notice. 'Have you ever heard that before?'

'No.'

'It's a nursery rhyme.'

'Is it?'

Susan paused. 'I can ride that horse, can't I?'

'You bet.'

'I'll go and call my mum.'

'OK.'

Prim crossed her fingers. Please God – let her agree, she prayed.

*

While Susan was telephoning, Prim decided to face Billy. She called him over, hoping Len wouldn't come as well. But of course he did.

'I don't want you,' said Prim recklessly. Len shrugged and walked away and she could see that she had hurt him. But she had to have this friend – at any cost.

'Billy—'

'You've upset him now.'

'I'm sorry.'

'You've really upset him.'

'I'll say sorry.'

He seemed only slightly appeased. 'You'd better. What do you want?'

'A favour.'

'Oh yeah?'

'A big one.'

'What is it?'

'I got me a friend.'

'Who?'

'Susan.'

'She's a Gorgio – she ain't your friend.'

'I can have one – Len had his mates in London.'

'So – you got a friend.' Billy didn't sound very interested.

Doesn't he know how important it is to me, she fumed. But she also knew that she had to be patient.

'I'm bringing her home.'

'When?'

'Tonight.'

'Blimey.' He stared at her in some amazement.

'What's wrong with that?'

'Nothing. What's the favour?'

'She wants to ride Blackie.'

'No chance.'

'Please—'

'No one rides Blackie.'

'Just this once.'

'No.'

'*Please*, Billy.' Her eyes were full of tears. 'I'll give you anything.'

'Even your honey-coloured stone?'

'The good luck one? That's my most precious. It's magic . . . oh, Billy—'

'She can't ride Blackie then.'

'All right.'

'You mean it?'

'I'll give it to you.'

'Forever?'

'Yes – forever.'

'I'll have to be around when she's riding.'

'OK. But, Billy—'

'Yeah?'

'Be nice to her.'

'OK. But you'd better speak to Len, or he'll give her a mouthful.'

'Len.' She approached him cautiously, within minutes of the bell, still frustratingly not knowing whether Susan's mum had agreed or not.

'What do *you* want?'

'I'm sorry I told you to go away.'

'I don't care. Now *you* go away.'

'Len, please ...' She had to calm him down somehow and it wasn't going to be easy. Once Len was in a mood, he was in a mood. 'Please help me.'

There must have been enough despair in her eyes to make him relent. Just a little.

'What do you want then?' he asked ungraciously.

'I'm bringing a friend home.'

'Gorgio?'

'It's not unknown.'

'Wish we knew more,' said Len unexpectedly.

'What?' Prim was amazed. But then she thought – why was she? He'd missed his London friends so much. 'Why didn't you ever bring those friends of yours home?' she asked.

'Didn't like to.'

'What do you mean?'

'Dunno. Maybe I felt they wouldn't fit in.'

'Will Susan?' Suddenly Prim was dependent on his opinion. And at the same time she was thinking – little scruff, who does he think he is?

'Her? You're bringing *her* home?'

'Yes.'

'You that desperate?'

She paused. 'Yes.'

'Why?'

'I want a friend. An outside friend. An outside friend I can bring home. Not like yours that you didn't want to.'

'But she's a bit thick, isn't she?'

'Thick? She's – she's good at work.'

'Thick – thick in a different kind of way.'

'I don't get you.'

'I can't tell you, but be careful, Prim. Just be careful.' He walked away, leaving Prim sensing that this was the most important conversation she had ever had with her little brother. But she couldn't for the life of her think why.


'Is this it?'

Prim nodded proudly.

'It's very crowded, isn't it?'

'Crowded?'

'With caravans and things. And all those old vehicles.'

'They tow the trailers.'

'I see.' Susan looked around doubtfully.

Just then Vi came up. 'Hallo, love. Brought a friend home?'

Good old Mum, thought Prim. Casual as ever. Whatever she thinks of Gorgios she'd never show it.

'This is Susan,' said Prim loudly, rather as if she had brought a rabbit home. She felt as if she owned her.

'Hallo, Susan. Like a cup of tea?'

Prim wondered if she would like Mum's strong, sweet tea. Probably not. Oh well, she thought, you can't win them all.

'Where's the horse?' asked Susan. 'I'd like to ride him now.'

'You asked Billy?' Mum sounded alarmed.

'He said yes.'

'Blimey.' Mum was astounded and showed it.

Hurriedly Prim said, 'We'll come back for tea, Mum.'

'OK.'

Prim led Susan off to Blackie. Billy was there, rather as if he was standing guard.

'Hi, Susan.'

Well, at least he had greeted her.

'Is this Blackie?' Susan sounded dismayed.

'This is Blackie.'

'I thought he'd be a pony.'

'We only have horses here.' Billy's voice was rock hard. 'Do you want to ride him or not?'

Susan nodded uneasily.

'I'll give you a bunk up then.'

Somehow he pushed her up and she sat there motionless, as if she was afraid to do anything at all.

'Ever ridden?' asked Billy.

'Oh, yes,' she said in a rather superior voice.

'Sure?'

'I've been to a riding stable.'

'All right then. Take him down the bottom of the orchard and come back.' Billy sounded cross so Susan dug her heels in sharply. 'And have a good time,' he added in a smooth voice.

'Come on!' said Susan and dug her heels in again but more hesitantly this time.

'More than that.' Billy's voice was sharp again.

At first it looked as if Blackie, as usual, was going to be uncooperative. Then he sprang into sudden motion – and began to trot down the orchard.

'Help,' shouted Susan.

'She couldn't ride a bike,' pronounced Billy.

'Do something – she'll fall off.'

'Blackie!' commanded Billy. 'Come back!'

Blackie gave a whinny of protest and, amidst renewed shouts from Susan, began to trot back. Then, he put his head down and Susan slid miserably to the ground.

'You don't know how to ride, do you?' accused Billy fiercely. 'In fact you haven't the foggiest. Why didn't you tell me? I could have started you off from scratch.'

Prim closed her eyes. She could sense what was coming.

'Of course I can ride,' she said. 'It's your rotten horse. It's not trained properly.'

'You're a right prat, aren't you?' began Billy. 'He's trained perfect.'

Susan got to her feet. 'I'm going home.' Susan walked away without looking back. Prim watched her go.

'Sorry,' said Billy. 'But she's a right—'

'I know she is,' replied Prim. She walked slowly back to the trailer to tell Mum that Susan wouldn't be staying for tea after all.

## 7    Deadly Yew

Prim avoided Susan for the rest of the week. Then, on Friday morning, Mrs Crimble called her in.

'Something rather odd's happened, Primrose.'

'Yes, miss?'

'Someone found another five pound note on the playing field.'

'They must be scattering them around.'

'It's very strange. Are you *sure* you found that note on the field?'

'Yes, miss.'

'Very well. But if no one claims this one I shall give it to Oxfam.'

Prim went home that evening very thoughtfully. There was a smell of autumn in the air and the leaves were coming off the trees in the orchard. They still didn't know if they could stay the winter. Mrs Pringle and her lawyers were battling away with the council, but no one could predict the outcome. Maybe it would be good to move on, thought Prim, as long as it wasn't back to that awful official site in London.

Yet she would miss the orchard and the community there. They were like one big family; bickering and squabbling sometimes, but it was their own world there amongst the lines of apple trees.

When Prim got back, she sought out Billy who, as usual, was with Blackie.

'Billy.'

'Yeah?'

'I want to talk.'

'More favours?'

'You done me enough.'

He looked relieved and friendly. 'Well then?'

'You know that money Gran gave me towards some new jeans?'

'Yeah.'

'It was a fiver, wasn't it?'

'I dunno.'

'Well, it was.'

'So what?'

'That was the fiver I gave back to Susan.'

'You mean—' Billy stared at her in gathering bewilderment. 'You mean—'

'Now the real one's been found on the field. Mrs Crimble told me.'

'You mean – you pretended to find it. And handed your own fiver in?'

'Yeah.'

'You're barmy.'

'Maybe I am.'

'Just to be friends with that stuck-up girl?'

'Something like that.'

'You're—'

'Don't say it again, Billy.'

'Sorry.'

'I'm not going to tell Mum.'

'What about Gran? And the jeans?'

'I've cleaned up my old pair – the pair I never liked. I'll have to wear them. She'll never notice.'

'Blimey.'

'So you think I'm a fool?'

Billy considered. 'No.'

'You mean you can see why?'

'You want a Gorgio mate. You'll do anything to get one,' summarised Billy rather bleakly.

'I *would* have done.'

'You mean – not now?'

'I don't care now. She was a dopey girl.'

'Just scared. Scared and proud. We're proud. Us lot.'

'Billy—' She paused. 'Don't you need a Gorgio mate?'

'No. Got mates here. And my Blackie.'

'You don't want one?'

He shook his head. 'No. No need.'

'What's to become of us then?' she asked with sudden distress.

'I'll go in the scrap with Dad. Might get a cart. Do a bit of totting with Blackie.'

'And Len?'

'He can come in with me if he behaves himself.'

'And me?'

'You? You'll marry. Have kids.'

'Thanks.'

'How many you going to have?'

'Shut up, Billy.'

That's all I got to look forward to then, thought Prim as she sat watching telly with Mum. Leave school. Get a bloke. Have kids. Blimey, she kept thinking over and over again, is that all? She glanced at Mum, knitting and watching the screen at the same time. That's what she always did. Mum and Dad – they had their rows, but they'd been together for a long time. Suddenly Prim had the overpowering urge to ask her.

'Mum?'

'Mm?'

'You happy?'

'Mm.'

'Mum – you're not listening!'

'What you say, love?'

'I said – are you happy?'

Mum turned to her in surprise. 'That's a funny question to ask.'

'Why?'

'I've never been unhappy – except in London. Life's been good to us. I've a good man. I'm free – still in a trailer, not in a house. And that's something to thank the Good Lord for.'

'So – when did you marry Dad?'

'When I was nineteen.'

'And what did you do before that?'

'Helped your gran – and waited for a bloke.'

'Is that what I'll do?'

'Course you will. All I can hope and pray is that Mrs Pringle wins her court case, and we can stay here for the rest of our lives.'

At that moment Reuben came in, tired and hungry. Vi got up to make his supper.

'Your daughter's asking a few questions,' she announced.

'Yeah?' He flung himself down in front of the television.

'Wants to know if I'm happy.'

'Your mum's never happy,' he muttered. 'Not unless she's having a go at me. Then she's happy.'

'Get on with you,' said Vi. 'You've got me to make your meals. What more do you want? I was just telling her, it's been a good enough life – helping Mum, marrying a lazy man. Still, you're all right if I get behind you!'

'And you're always there,' laughed Reuben.

Prim found the whole conversation rather depressing. And she showed it.

'Well, my girl,' said Reuben, suddenly swinging away from the television. 'And just what's going to turn you on that we ain't got?'

'It's not that, Dad. I just want to take a look around me.'

'Do that. And what do you see? A good family,

making good money.' He laughed but Prim caught the sudden uneasy mood in him that she had started.

'It's not that, Dad. It's me. I don't want to kick around after school, waiting to get married. Waiting for some bloke. Some Rom.'

'What do you want then?' he asked aggressively.

'See a bit of the world. I'd like to – go to Paris.'

'You would, would you? And where do you think the money's coming from for that?'

'I'll earn it.'

'Doing what?'

'I'll get myself a trade.'

'Yeah? You haven't got the muscle for the scrap.'

'Haven't I? I'm stronger than you think.'

'Yeah?' He turned back to the screen.

'Dad—'

'What now?'

'Would you try me?'

'Eh?'

'Would you try me on the scrap?'

'Give over.'

'Come on, my girl,' said Vi. 'Leave your dad alone. He's tired.'

'Why won't he try me?'

'It's not the way.'

'The way?' Her voice was scoffing. 'What way?'

'Women have their way; men theirs. That's our life.'

'Well, it's time for a change.'

'Right little women's libber.' Reuben chuckled.

'Please let me – let me have a try just for one day. Then if I'm no good, you can tell me to get lost.'

'No,' said Reuben, his eyes glued to the screen. 'And that's my final word.'

The door opened and Billy poked his head in. He looked very upset.

'Dad.'

'What now?'

'It's Blackie. He's lying down in the wood – and he won't move.'

Supper was abandoned as the Roberts hurried to the wood. Len was already there, leaning over Blackie who was rolling over and over on the ground.

'He's bad,' said Len.

'He's eaten yew,' said a voice. It was Tommy Smith, one of the other Travellers in the orchard. He often helped Billy with Blackie and had once, reputedly, been a horse breeder himself. 'I told you not to let him in the wood, Billy, he can get through to the old yew hedge that way.'

'He wandered off.'

'He should have been tied up.'

'I know,' wailed Billy. 'What we going to do, Dad?'

'He'll need a vet,' said Reuben turning to Tommy, who was looking gloomily down at Blackie.

'Well, it's a long shot.'

'What do you mean?' demanded Billy. 'A long shot?'

'Yew's a very poisonous tree, boy. And it's quick acting.'

'My Blackie's not going to die,' yelled Billy with sudden aggression.

'Yew's very poisonous—' began Tommy again.

But Len cut him short fiercely. 'Course Blackie's not going to die, Billy. We had the vet before. What's his name – Timber or something?'

'Wood,' said Vi firmly. 'Graham Wood. I'll go up to Mrs Pringle's and ring him.'

She hurried off. Billy knelt down by the horse and began to stroke his head. There was foam on his lips and sweat all over his body.

'Don't look too good to me,' said Tommy.

Prim wished he'd go away.

Mum didn't come back for a long time and eventually Prim went to look for her. She was standing in Mrs Pringle's hallway, thumbing through the telephone directory hopelessly.

'It's no good, Mum. You can't *read*.'

'I can recognise the shape of a name sometimes,' Vi said defensively.

Prim glanced at the page. 'You're looking under Butcher.' Her voice was blunt. 'Can't you remember the vet's number? You've always had such a good memory.'

'He's out,' she said miserably.

'Oh.' Prim looked up Vet in the Yellow Pages and tried a couple of numbers. The first was out, the second away. And there were no more vets.

97

'Now what we going to do?' wailed Vi.

Something clicked in Prim's mind. 'Susan,' she said.

'Eh?'

'Susan's dad. He's a vet. Over in Canterbury. He wouldn't be in this book.'

'Well, ring her.'

It was going to be difficult, thought Prim, after all that had happened. But then Blackie was dying, wasn't he?

'It'll be all right,' said Vi encouragingly. 'OK, Blackie threw her, but she's not going to hold that against us, is she?'

Prim wasn't so sure as she fearfully dialled Susan's number. As luck would have it, Susan answered.

'It's Prim.'

'Oh, yes?' Her voice was polite but uninterested.

'We got trouble.'

'Sorry?'

'Trouble with Blackie.'

'The horse?'

'Yeah, he's eaten yew.'

'What?'

'It's poisonous. He's very ill. Might die.'

'I'm very sorry.' Her voice was still cold. 'Why are you phoning me?'

'Because your dad's a vet. You said he was once.'

'Oh he's not an actual vet. He lectures in veterinary surgery.'

'Oh.' Prim's heart sank. 'We phoned all the other vets. They're either out or away.'

'I'm afraid my father's asleep.'

'Anyway, you said he can't help.'

'He *was* a vet.'

'Does he know what to do?' Prim's voice was desperate.

'Of course he does.'

'Then—'

'He's asleep.'

'Susan – Blackie's dying.'

'Look, I'd like to help—' Susan's voice tailed away.

'Hang on, I'm coming round.'

'You're *what*—?'

But Prim put the phone down with a click. 'Mum, we got a chance. Go and tell Billy I'm bringing a vet. Tell him to get Blackie to hang on.'


Prim knocked gingerly on the door. Susan opened it, equally tentatively.

'It's you.'

'Yeah, I said I'd come.'

'We *can't* help – I told you.'

'Your dad's a vet.'

'He's—'

'Asleep. You told me that too. So I'm going to wake him up.'

'You can't.'

'You stand aside – or I'll push you out of the way.'

'You're invading—'

'Blackie's dying. Now, you gonna let me in or not?'

Susan stood back meekly.

'Go and wake him up,' commanded Prim. 'And hurry!'

Prim waited in the lounge. She felt she could hardly breathe despite the fact that the room was large and airy. Somehow the ceiling seemed very low and the walls too near. Also, she was very nervous. Suppose Susan's father refused to come? Blackie would die. Then she heard two pairs of feet descending the stairs and her breathing became shorter.

The door opened and a fat, jolly man came into the room in a dressing-gown. He wore glasses, and although he looked tired he was smiling. Prim felt a slight sense of relief.

'Hallo, young lady. I hear you've got a problem.'

'Our Blackie's dying.' There was a sob in her voice.

'A horse? What happened to him?'

'He's eaten yew.'

'Ah.'

'Will you help us?'

'Of course I will – I'll come straight away. I'm sorry I was in bed. I've got a long drive tomorrow.'

'I'm sorry.'

He came up to Prim and put his hands on her shoulders. Looking down at her with almost unbearable kindness he said, 'I'll be ready in five minutes. And don't give up hope. I've got some drugs that should help.'

Prim could have cried with relief. In fact she almost

did. Particularly when Susan said, 'Can I come too?'
And her voice was no longer cold.

Having given Blackie his injection, he looked up at
Billy kindly.

'He'll be all right. Keep walking him. Don't let him
roll. Put a blanket over him and keep him warm till
the sweating stops.'

'Is he really going to be all right, mister?' asked
Billy fiercely.

'He's going to be fine.'

'Thanks for coming.' Reuben took out his wallet.
'How much do we owe you?'

'Nothing.'

'What?'

'I said nothing. I'm not a practising vet – although
I keep some stuff still in the old surgery. Never know
when it might come in useful.'

'Cup of tea, sir?' asked Vi.

'Well, I'd better—' Then he paused and looked
round at their expectant faces. 'I wouldn't say no,' he
said.

'Your dad's great,' said Prim as she sat with Susan on
the steps of the trailer.

'Yes, but *I'm* sorry.'

'What for?' Prim was genuinely puzzled.

'For the way I've behaved.'

'Rubbish.'

'But it's true. I should never have told Billy I could
ride.'

'You were proud.'

'Too proud. I've only been to the stables a couple of times. But you lot ... seemed so sure of yourselves. I s'pose I wanted to prove something.'

'It doesn't matter.' Prim looked down hurriedly.

'It does. Will you come to tea with me?'

'I don't—'

'Please.'

'You sure?'

'Yes. We could be friends – if you'd like.'

Prim considered. She'd really given up the idea of having a Gorgio friend. Did she want one now? Then she remembered her conversation with Mum and Dad. Well – she was being educated, wasn't she? Maybe if she knew some Gorgios she'd get to Paris. Eventually.

'All right then.'

'Would Billy – ever teach me to ride Blackie?'

'It's not for that, is it?'

'No. It never was. I was curious about you – a bit frightened.'

'Why?'

'You're different.'

'Yeah ...' Prim smiled. 'If you chat him up, Billy might.'

'It doesn't matter if he doesn't,' said Susan. 'I still want to be friends.'

# 8 *Running Away*

Mrs Pringle was in tears. 'We've lost,' she said. Vi and Len stared at her in amazement. They had almost forgotten the long drawn-out battle she had been having with the council over whether or not their trailers could stay in her orchard.

'Lost?'

'I've tried everything. But they say you've got to go by the end of the month or they'll fine me so much money that I'll have to sell up.' She continued to cry. 'What am I going to *do*?'

'You'll do nothing,' said Vi. 'We'll have to go.' Her voice shook and Len clutched at her hand. For once he wasn't aggressive, didn't suggest they stay and fight. And as for Vi – all she could see were the London streets, though it wasn't even certain they could go back there. The only alternative was a roadside, a lay-by somewhere with traffic thundering past and lights continually flashing through the trailer windows. And it wasn't just them, it was the other families in the orchard. Then Vi thought of something.

'Does this apply to the scrapyard?'

Mrs Pringle smiled. 'I didn't tell them about that – and they didn't look.'

'Good for you. But they *will* find out, and that's another change of use you haven't applied for.'

'At least you can have it until they do.' Mrs Pringle sniffed.

Vi was suddenly surprised again; usually Mrs Pringle rambled away, but it would seem that if a crisis occurred she was able to pull herself together. Sadly, it looked as if this would be the final crisis.

'Mrs P,' said Len.

'Yes, my dear?'

'Thanks for everything.'

Mrs Pringle began to cry all over again.

It took a day or so for the news to really sink in amongst the families in the orchard. Reuben and Vi spent hours with them, trying to sort out their futures. Then, one evening, Reuben called a family conference. They all sat gloomily in the trailer, wondering what he was going to say. But before Reuben spoke, Len put in, 'Dad.'

'Well?'

'I don't want my London mates any more. We're beginning to make friends at school now.'

'And I've got Susan,' said Prim.

'And I've got Blackie.' Billy sounded helpless. 'I don't want him to go back to Bubbles.'

'OK,' said Reuben quietly. 'Now hear me out. I

don't want to go back to London either. And anyway – the site's full up. And so is every other official site all over the county. I've checked and yesterday I drove to each one. It wasn't much of an effort as there aren't many. And anyway, even in the country the official sites have got a warden and rules and so on.'

'We don't want that,' said Len.

'We don't. But what else is there?'

'Not the roadside again,' pleaded Vi. 'Not with all them lights and noise.'

'I don't want that either. There's just one possibility . . . but it means splitting up from the others.'

'Staying on our own?' said Vi doubtfully. 'What about the old people?'

Reuben shook his head. 'They'll have to go back to Silas.'

'They won't like that.'

'They'll have to lump it.'

'If we're going to be alone, Dad,' said Billy slowly. 'What about Blackie?'

'There's room for him. But it means pulling together. The scrapyard up here will close anyway; they're all off to different places, relatives mostly. We won't have enough labour, and anyway Mrs P would soon have to get rid of us, even from there.'

'So what's going to happen, Dad?' asked Prim quietly.

'Last night, just before it got dark, I found this tiny wood. Just off a B road at Tineham. It's got a load of junk in it, but we could clear that – like we cleared here.'

'But who does it belong to?' asked Vi.

'That's the joy of it – no one.'

'How do you know?'

'I went into the pub and asked. The landlord said it's part of Tineham Common.'

'Squatters' rights?' asked Vi.

'No, we got no rights. But we might not be disturbed there. Other Travellers have been before us, there's a hell of a mess. But if we cleaned that up . . .'

'You mean the council – it would look good to them?' There was a little more hope in Vi's voice now.

'Yeah.'

'But what about cutting up the scrap?'

'There's a valley – very small and well out of sight. But there's a track down to it that would take the truck. Only one thing . . .' He paused, nervously for him. 'I'm going to be on my own. I'll need help.'

'I'll go with you, Dad.' Len was immediately enthusiastic.

Reuben shook his head. 'You're not big enough yet, boy.' There was a long silence as he turned to Billy. 'Well, Bill?'

The silence lengthened. 'No, Dad,' said Billy at last.

'What?'

'I said no. I want to finish my education. I have to.

106

I can't do all that reading and writing well enough yet, Dad.'

'You can do that at home.'

'No, I couldn't.'

'Get one of them home tutors.'

'No, Dad. I want to stay at school. You can't make me.'

The rest of the family were amazed. They had never heard Billy so determined before.

'Don't you see, Bill?' intervened Vi. 'Your dad can't do it on his own.'

'He'll have to find someone.'

'Billy – we're all splitting up.'

'I know. I can't, Mum.' He was conscious of them all staring at him in hostility, but their hostility was matched by surprise. They had never heard him speak – nor act – like this before. They were looking at him as if he was a stranger.

'Dad, you wanted me to go to school.' Billy tried to explain, knowing that what he was going to say was hopeless. 'You wanted me to go to school to learn. I haven't finished learning yet.'

'You've learnt enough,' said Reuben grimly.

'No, Dad. I haven't. Not nearly enough.' And as Billy spoke he became more and more convinced he was right.

'You want to learn too much,' spluttered Len. 'Soon you'll be too good for us.'

'You shut up.'

'Make me!'

107

'I'll punch your face in.'

'Bet you can't.'

Billy got up to hit Len – and then he sat down again. It wasn't worth the effort.

'Billy, I understand about the school,' said Prim. She turned to her father. 'Why don't you take me, Dad – I'll work with you.'

'No.'

'But why not? I told you I was strong. I can prove it.'

'It's not our way.'

'That's just old-fashioned.'

'No it's not, girl. It's the right way. The eldest boy.'

'I told you, Dad,' said Billy. 'I want to stay at school.'

Reuben got up. 'I could beat you – I should beat you.'

'It wouldn't change anything.'

'I'll give you a final chance, Bill.' Reuben was white under his leathery tan, but whether it was from rage or rejection it was hard to say.

'No.'

'Then get out.'

'*What?*'

'Get out. And take your horse with you.'

'Reuben – he's just thirteen. Thirteen years old!' Vi was on her feet.

'So?'

'You can't *do* this.'

108

'He's taken against our ways – taken against his father.'

'I haven't, Dad.'

'Get out!'

'All right.' Billy stood up.

Vi began to cry. 'Reuben, for God's sake.'

Len and Prim were so shocked that they just stood there, staring at their father in horror.

'Where's he going to go?' asked Len eventually, his eyes full of tears.

There was silence.

'Where you going to go, Bill?' Len turned to his brother, the tears running down his grubby cheeks, making white trails.

'No problem.'

'What do you mean?' demanded Prim.

'I'll go down the fair.'

'Uncle Jim's?'

'He's no uncle,' snapped Reuben. 'We're not related to Showmen.'

'Don't be a fool.' Vi's voice was very cold. 'Jim's a good man.'

'It's down at Barney's Bottom – they're going to winter there. He's got a yard and all – and I got real friendly with his Wayne. They'll put me up at the yard, and I can work for him in the evenings and weekends. Earn me keep, and still go to school.'

'How do you know Jim'll take you?' asked Prim.

'I can try.'

'What about Blackie?' demanded Len.

'I'll take him with me. They'll find room there. Jim's got a couple of horses.'

'No,' said Vi. 'You're not going anywhere.' She stared angrily at her husband. 'Take it back, Reuben. Make it right for the boy.'

Reuben got up. 'Either Billy boy works for his dad – or he gets out. That's my final word.' Then he walked slowly away.

'Sorry, Mum. I'll go and see if Uncle Jim will have me. If he will I'll come back and get Blackie.'

'And if he doesn't?'

'I'll think of something else.'

'Bill – think it over,' Prim began, while Len sobbed on his bunk.

'Is school *that* important?' asked Vi. 'Important enough to break up the family?'

'It's my future, Mum,' he said and walked to the door of the trailer.

'Is it more important than being a Rom?' continued Vi.

'Nothing's more important than being a Rom,' said Billy with total conviction. 'But what's the use of not being able to read and write. Real proper. Us lot need it more than ever. I'll see you later.'

Uncle Jim was young and his rough kindness was almost too much for Billy after the scene at home, and for a moment he was terrified that he was going to cry.

'Course you can stay, Bill – if you don't mind

110

sleeping in with Wayne. And Blackie can go in the field. Only thing is, I don't want to fall out with your dad. So you'll try and patch it up with him, won't you?'

'He'll have to patch it up with me,' replied Billy stubbornly.

'Give him the chance then.'

'If it comes up.'

'OK – now about the work. This is our winter quarters, see, and there's a lot to do. Most of the families with the rides aren't in yet, but I've had to bring the cars back for a while. They haven't been looked at for months now, so if you can give me and Wayne a bit of a hand that would be great. I'll pay you.'

'I won't need much.'

'I'll give you the going rate, Bill. Wayne tells me you're a good worker.'

'How does he know?' muttered Billy. He was beginning to feel very homesick already and he'd only been here ten minutes! Maybe when he fetched Blackie it would be better. But he knew in his heart of hearts that it wouldn't.

'Takes one to know one,' grinned Wayne. He was a little imp of a boy, small for his age but tough. The Showmen weren't Romany so he wasn't dark. He had fair hair and bright blue eyes that sparkled with fun. That was what Billy had always liked about him. Wayne was so alive.

'But do us a favour,' repeated Jim.

111

'What's that?'

'Give your dad a chance.'

'It's not easy. He doesn't understand.'

'That's what all kids say.'

'About going to school.'

'You could think about that, young Wayne.' His father turned to him. 'It's any excuse with you.'

'I don't like school,' said Wayne.

'Neither do I much,' agreed Billy. 'But I got to learn.'

The next few days were the worst Billy and his family had ever experienced. Billy went to school every day from the winter quarters, where he saw his sister and brother – both of whom continuously tried to persuade him to come home. But he remained unmoved, determined that he would win the battle with his father. For Billy knew that once he gave in he would never learn anything again – except how to extract metals from car parts and sell them. He only had the haziest idea of what he was going to do when he grew up, but he hoped it could be something to do with horses and still connected with the Travelling life. He had no wish to change; no wish to become a Gorgio.

But when he returned to the fairground's winter quarters his homesickness was continually with him – a nagging ache that never let him forget what he had left. In fact Vi came to see him every day, but as she spent most of her time pleading in vain with him to come back, this meant more aching, more pain.

In the orchard, Billy was deeply missed. Prim could hardly bear to come home, Len uncharacteristically rarely spoke and Vi was continually bad-tempered. Reuben worked in the yard until the light faded, and then went to the pub. He would return at closing time, staggering slightly, eat the bread and cheese Vi had left out for him and then tumble heavily into bed. He woke up the next morning with a hangover, grabbed a cup of tea and went out early to work, so that he wouldn't have to talk to anyone. He never made any reference to their new home, and although it was coming up to the end of October, he never mentioned moving or made any plans to do so. Autumnal winds shook the apple trees and then fruit began to fall, rotting on the ground.

In any spare time he had, which was not much, Billy rode Blackie and played football with Wayne. Despite his liveliness, Wayne was an understanding companion and didn't press Billy to talk or to do anything that he didn't want to do. He just kept him company, and for this Billy was grateful.

After Billy had been gone five days, Len had an idea – a private idea that he didn't want anyone to share. It might work, he thought. If it didn't he would be in big trouble, but he didn't think that Billy would be any the worse off. Anyway it was definitely worth giving it a swing. That afternoon he came back home from school in a very nervous mood, and hurried straight down to the scrapyard. When he saw his dad his nerve almost failed. But not quite.

'Dad.'

'What do you want?' He was hauling an engine out of an ancient Ford with a hoist. Silas Penfold was helping him.

'Billy's hurt.'

'What?'

'Hurt.'

'How?'

'Got his arm trapped in one of them dodgems. They're trying to get him free.'

'My Billy. God no – not my Billy.' His father's shock was so great that a terrible wave of fear coursed through Len's whole being. Reuben began to shake, then pulled himself together. 'Take me to him – we'll go in the van. Fast.'

'Dad?' Billy was polishing up one of the dodgem cars after it had been repainted. But he had no time to say anything else as Reuben threw his arms round him and hugged him so tight that he could hardly breathe. Then Reuben remembered something and he jumped away.

'Your arm, Bill.'

'Arm?'

'You're hurt – you hurt your arm.' Then he moved forward, looking intently at Billy's arm. 'It looks – where does it hurt?'

'I don't know what you're on about. My arm's fine.'

'But – Len told me you'd had an accident – an accident to your arm.'

'I've had no accident. Len must have popped his—'

They both turned on Len, who backed away. Reuben's voice was a roar that brought Uncle Jim and Wayne running up.

'*Len!*'

'Dad – I – Dad—'

'Len! What the hell have you got to say for yourself?'

'Not a lot.'

'What did you say?'

'I mean – it was worth a try – bringing you two together.'

Uncle Jim laughed, and then hurriedly turned the laugh into a cough as Wayne merely gasped.

'You made it up!' yelled Reuben. 'You made it up that Billy had had an accident?'

'Yes, Dad.'

'I'll take you apart. Later.' Something in Reuben's face altered. 'Bill – I found me a partner. Silas Penfold. And I'm sorry – I been thinking . . . I do understand—'

'You mean—'

'Come back, boy. Please come back. I'll do anything to get you back. I'll even go easy on Len.'

Billy grinned. 'That won't get me back, Dad.'

Len gave a terrible wail. 'You can't say that – not after all I done for you!'

# 9  *Moving On Again*

'And this is for you, Mrs P.'

'For me, dear?'

'From all of us Roms.'

Mrs Pringle was standing in her exceedingly dusty drawing-room. She was in one of her vague moods. Maybe she is on purpose, thought Vi. Maybe she can't bear it.

'Oh, it's lovely.'

'Grandad made it,' said Reuben.

The little old man came up and shook her hand.

'Mr Roberts?'

'Ah.'

'The older Mr Roberts?' Mrs Pringle seemed to be temporarily less vague as she looked down at the beautifully carved miniature vardo he had given her. 'It's so beautiful – exquisite.'

The room was full of the five families and their children. It was a touching but awkward little ceremony.

'It's because we had such a good home here,' said one of the Travelling women. 'Maybe we haven't been here very long, but it was good. And you fought for us. So if you're ever in trouble, Mrs Pringle, you can be sure the Travellers will help you.'

'I'm always in trouble,' said Mrs Pringle sadly. 'And I shall miss you.'

'What will you do with the orchard?' asked Prim.

'I'm going to restore the trees,' said Mrs Pringle. 'In memory of my Travellers. Perhaps you'll come and help pick the apples next year.'

'You bet we will,' said Len.

The wood was a major disappointment. And because of Billy's dispute with his father there had been no time for the Roberts to try to clean it up before they moved in. The whole place was much worse than the orchard, with old bedsteads, bicycle wheels, tyres, car wrecks, prams – even a large kitchen table and chest of drawers.

Somehow the Roberts managed to get the two trailers in, plus the truck and van. Blackie came last, looking rather put out. But the reunion of Billy and Reuben had given the family a tremendous boost and they set to work, clearing the wood with considerable energy. While they were doing it, Prim started to pull apart what she thought was a bunch of old rags at the very back of the wood. But as she did so, it began to move. Then the rags stood up.

Prim continued to scream until the others raced up, headed by Len.

'Blimey,' he said. 'Are you a tramp?'

He was looking at a very old, very dishevelled man with a long dirty white beard and equally unkempt long hair.

'I'm a man of the road,' he said in a dignified if cracked voice.

'What's your name?' gasped Prim.

'Benjamin Arthur Warrington-Butts. And you're in my wood.'

'Your wood?' Reuben's voice was hesitant. 'I didn't think it was anyone's wood.'

'Squatters' rights.'

'Ah.'

'You live here?' asked Len.

'Got a hut. Couple of hundred yards away.'

'But I thought that was a private estate,' said Reuben.

'I'm just outside their boundaries.' He gave a wheezy laugh. 'They're good for a rabbit or two.'

'You a poacher?' asked Len with burning interest.

'I do me bit.'

'Well, I don't suppose we'll disturb each other,' said Reuben firmly. 'Will we?'

Benjamin Arthur Warrington-Butts considered. 'I'm a bit of a hermit.'

'We'll respect that,' said Vi. She meant it; she could smell him from where she stood.

'Course I like a bit of company once in a while. And maybe a bath. And a bite to eat.' He looked at Vi calculatingly.

'We can supply all that,' said Reuben and Vi sighed. 'But don't go getting us into trouble. Not with your poaching.'

'My dear fellow.' Really, he had quite an educated voice, thought Prim. 'I wouldn't dream of it.'

'It's easy to do,' said Reuben shortly.

'How long you been on the road then?' asked Len with his usual nosiness.

'Shut up, Len,' hissed Billy.

'No, I like a little curiosity. I've been on the road for twenty years, young feller. Ever since the wife walked out.'

'I'm sorry,' said Prim.

'I was delighted to see her go. I always was a bit of a wanderer. Used to be in Africa – selling tea-cloths.'

'Tea-cloths?' Was he kidding, wondered Prim. But he quickly changed the subject.

'Call me Ben,' he said. 'If you'd like to.'

'All right, Ben,' said Vi. 'We'll be friends. But we won't get each other into trouble. That's the bargain.'

Ben smiled graciously. 'That's the bargain, madam. May I know your name? Or would you prefer . . .'

Vi began to introduce them all. As she did so, Billy watched Len watching Ben. He was staring at him admiringly. Billy knew that Ben had made a conquest. And that worried him.

'Rabbit, madam?'

'Oh—'

'Compliments of the wood.'

Vi looked at Ben suspiciously. 'Where did you get it?'

'Butcher's?'

'Ben, where did you get it?'

He nodded over his shoulder.

'Not in the private park?'

'No, Vi. What do you think I am? A poacher?'

Len, who was starting to hang around with the old man, piped up: 'Honest, Mum – it wasn't—'

'You were with him?'

'He's got a few snares.'

'Just showing the lad a bit of woodcraft.'

'I'd rather you didn't.'

'Sorry, Vi.'

'But, Mum—'

'Shut up, Len.' Vi strode away, showing the rabbit en route to Reuben and Silas, who regularly came from a place the Penfolds had found to help him cut up scrap. Reuben grinned and then the smile slowly vanished from his face as Vi shouted something at him.

'I'm not in favour,' said Ben sadly.

Prim grinned at him. 'You're all right – providing you don't lead my little brother astray.'

'Susan!' Prim was delighted.

'Thought I'd come and see how you were all getting on.'

'It's great you've come.'

'This wood looks lovely now – it used to look awful.'

'We really worked to clean it up, and you can't even see the scrap. Well, not really. It's down in the little valley.'

'I think it's all smashing. You've done the place a service. Who's that?' She paused uneasily, watching Ben and Len walking off together.

'An old tramp. He's harmless.'

'Does he always wear that long black coat? He looks like an out-of-work undertaker.'

'That's his best. He usually looks much worse.'

'Does he smell?' asked Susan, shuddering.

'Quite a bit.'

'Want a ride on Blackie?' asked Billy, strolling up.

Susan flushed. 'I'm not good enough—'

'Come on. I'll give you a lesson. Or are you scared?'

'I'm not scared.'

'Come on then.'

'I'll make some tea,' said Prim.

Prim and her mother were just brewing up when Len came rushing in, looking panicky.

'The coppers are here.'

Vi dropped a cup, cursing as it smashed in the sink. 'Now what?' She opened the door to see two young policemen strolling up the woodland path.

'Afternoon, Mrs—'

'Roberts.'

'Thought we'd ask you a few questions. Is that OK?'

121

It was always the same, thought Prim. One asked the questions, the other looked around. Didn't they ever change their training methods?

'Come in.'

'Thanks.'

They mounted the steps, blinked their way into the interior and hovered awkwardly.

'Sit down.'

They sat down, equally awkwardly, side by side on the sofa.

'Can I help you?' She poured out two mugs of scalding sweet tea and they took them like clumsy schoolboys.

'You been here long?' asked the talking policeman.

'It's common land.'

'Been long on it?'

'A week or so.'

'Right. Thinking of staying?'

'I told you – it's common land. We can stay here as long as we like.'

Prim closed her eyes. She wished her mother wouldn't be so defensive. Obviously so did the talking policeman. But he was kind rather than patronising.

'No need to worry, love. We're not here to look into all that.'

'What then?'

'Just been a lot of poaching round here lately.'

'Oh yes?'

'On the Knight estate.'

122

'Where's that?'

'Half a mile into the woods. It's fenced off.'

'We wouldn't go in there. Or anywhere else come to that. We don't poach.'

Oh dear, thought Prim. But maybe Dad would have been worse.

'I'm not saying you would, love. What about the old boy?'

'Who?'

'The tramp.'

'Oh, him – he don't poach either.'

That moment the policeman's eyes were drawn to the rabbit lying on the table. Prim decided to act quickly.

'He gave it to us.'

'The tramp?'

'Yeah. Ben. But he said he – found it this side of the fence.'

'Did he now? We ran into him up the road. Walking into the village.'

'Oh yeah.'

'He had a kid with him.'

'That's our Len.'

'He goes around with him?'

'Live and let live.'

'Yes. We know Benjamin, of course. If I were you, Mrs Roberts, I'd keep your boy away from him.'

'Why?'

'He's a poacher, Mrs Roberts. We just don't have enough evidence right now.'

Vi drew in her breath. 'All right,' she said. 'I'll speak to my boy.'

The two policemen got up to go, the silent one speaking at last. 'Thanks for the tea,' he said.

'So you're the shy one, are you?' Vi asked brusquely.

'Oh yes, m'am,' he replied. 'I wouldn't say boo to a goose. But I bet your kid Len would.'

'What do you mean by that?' asked Vi suspiciously.

'He's a bold little lad, I'll be bound. It would be a pity if he got into trouble with the law.'

'Yes,' said Vi. 'But don't worry – he won't.'


'Len!'

Vi furiously pushed past Susan as Len came back alone.

'Yes, Mum?' His voice was all innocence and surprise.

'Come in the trailer. Now.'

'What's up?' asked Susan. She had had a successful riding lesson with Billy, and Blackie had actually co-operated. As a result she was feeling much more confident.

'Oh, Len's in trouble as usual.'

'I love your brothers,' said Susan. 'They've got spirit, haven't they?'

'Yes, I suppose they have.'

'And I like it here – in this wood. It's so . . . cosy. Magical somehow – you all living here.'

'With Ben,' said Prim acidly.

'Oh – the tramp.'

'Anyway, let Mum bawl Len out for five minutes and then we'll go and have some tea.'

'What did the police want?' Susan asked hesitantly.

'They're after poachers. I don't think they suspect us. But Ben, they're certainly on to him, and Len keeps going with him.'

'Poaching on Mr Knight's land?'

'Yes.'

'We know Mr Knight.'

'Do you?' asked Prim fearfully. 'What's he like?'

'Tough,' replied Susan.


'Where's Len?'

'What?'

'Bill, where's Len?' hissed Reuben.

Billy looked at his watch. It was after three. 'He's here – below me. All tucked up. Why?'

'Thought I heard the sound of a car engine.'

'He's not going to drive away, is he, Dad?'

'Don't try to be funny. Check him out.'

Billy reached down. 'Yes, he's – hang on—'

'What's up?'

'There's a bolster here. No Len.'

'Gawd – the little . . . You know where he's gone, don't you?'

'Ben.'

'After all his mother said. 'Vi!'

'Yeah?' Her voice was sleepy.

'What's happening?' asked Prim equally sleepy.

'Len's gone,' hissed Reuben. 'Poaching.'

'That car engine ...' Billy suddenly realised something.

'Yes?' snapped his father impatiently.

'Could be the coppers.'

'I'll get them,' said Reuben.

'I'm coming too,' whispered Vi, Prim and Billy.

'No, you're not. I'm just taking Billy.'

'Why do you always leave women out?' hissed Prim angrily.

'This isn't the time to argue.' He cautiously lifted the curtain on the side window and then the one at the back. 'No sign of anyone. That car – maybe it was passing.'

'They could have hidden it somewhere,' said Vi.

'We're going to get that little sod back. Come on, Bill.'

And they were out of the trailer before either of the two women could argue. Then Reuben put his head back in.

'Don't put any lights on for gawd's sake.' And he disappeared.

'What does he think we are?' complained Vi. 'Idiots?'

'He thinks all women are idiots,' snapped Prim angrily.

Reuben crept forward and Billy followed. The wood seemed suspended in silence and every tiny sound made was like gunfire. Getting used to the stillness, they moved on towards the fence that separated the common land from the Knight wood.

Then Reuben signalled Billy to crouch down beside him.

'They're through the wire.'

'How do you know?'

'Look.' One strand had definitely been bent up.

'Yeah,' breathed Billy. 'What do we do?'

'Go after them.'

'Suppose—'

'The police? We got to risk it. For Len. We have to get him back. You game?'

'Sure.'

'OK. Follow me. Quietly.'

They climbed through the wire and went on, moving cautiously through the wood. It seemed much thicker this side.

'Wait.' Reuben grabbed Billy's arm.

'What?'

'There. A light.'

Reuben and Billy crept towards it.

The old man was fiddling with something on the ground while Len held a shaded lamp over him. Billy knew Len's expression of old – a kind of heady excitement. That was what he did it for, he knew that. The excitement of the night. They crept on until they were as near as they could get to them. Then Reuben sprang quietly out.

'Oi.'

'Gawd – my heart.' Ben clutched vaguely at his ragged chest and Len almost dropped the lamp.

'Dad,' he stuttered.

'Yes, and your brother Bill.'

'You prat, Len,' hissed Billy.

'You gave me a—'

'Be quiet!' Reuben's voice was steel. 'How dare you disobey your mother.'

'I never—'

'You were told not to go out. With him.'

Reuben and Billy looked down at the snare. It was empty.

'We was just laying—' began the old man in a nasal whine.

'You've taken my son on a criminal— what the hell—?'

A strong light shone out from a clump of bushes, completely dazzling them. Then another from the other side.

'Fair cop, I reckon,' said the talking policeman.

The silent one said nothing. But he grinned.

'I never thought I'd live to see the day,' said Vi, looking up at the low ceiling of the council house.

'It's temporary,' said Reuben. 'Temporary. We're lucky to be here. And not inside.' He glanced at Len who, although he'd had a terrible shock, was getting used to family criticism now. He'd made an appearance in juvenile court along with Billy, but they had both been bound over. Reuben, in his own court appearance, had been fined and Ben, because he had had so many other poaching offences, went to prison for six months. He had seemed to welcome it, however, and had told Reuben before being sentenced that 'now the winter's coming – I don't mind going inside for a bit'.

But, worse than anything, they had been evicted from the wood by the Local Authority and, as there were no other places to be found for them, a council house was produced in the most run-down part of the estate.

'You lost us our home, and made us move into a

house for the first time in our lives,' Reuben had accused Len. 'Just for a bit of selfish excitement.'

But Vi, Prim and Billy were more forgiving, for they knew that Len just couldn't take any more criticism. He was as miserable as they were about moving into a house.

'Will it really be temporary?' asked Billy. Blackie was over at the Penfolds and it was only a step down the road to visit him, but it wasn't like having him around all the time. The Penfolds had been lucky and managed to move on to another bit of common land from which no one had as yet said they had to go. So the scrap had been transferred there, and the trailers squeezed into a corner, but if the Penfolds were told to move on, the Roberts would not only lose their livelihood but maybe their trailers as well. It was the most desperate time of their lives.

'Yes, son. We'll be out in a few days.' Reuben was sweating and his clothes hung limply on him.

'Days?' Vi swung round on him furiously. 'Be realistic.'

'Twenty-four hours.'

'Don't be such a fool – we could be here weeks. Months.'

'No – twenty-four hours.' The sweat was standing out on his forehead, although the November morning was cold and raw.

'Are you all right, Dad?' asked Billy anxiously.

He nodded. 'I'm fine.'

'You got a temperature?' Prim felt his brow. 'You're boiling.'

'I'm OK. Listen, it's being inside a house. It's terrible. I never thought it would be as bad as this.'

'You've been in people's houses before,' snapped Vi.

'Never my own – but I'm not staying.'

'You what?'

'I know somewhere we could go.'

'Where?' said Len demandingly.

'It's a long way. I'm going to check it out. When I get back—'

'When will that be?' asked Vi suspiciously.

'Late tomorrow night.'

'You mean – you'll be leaving us that long?'

'I'll be back.'

'You're not thinking of dumping me here and walking out on me, are you, Reuben Roberts?' Her voice shook.

Reuben went over and kissed her. 'How long have we been married? Twenty years or more? I'll never leave you, Vi.'

'I should think not,' she sniffed. 'But why have you just thought of this place?'

'Because it's a long way – and I'll have to get another partner.'

'Dad.'

'Yes, Bill?'

'I'll work with you.'

'*What?*' Reuben seemed dazed.

'*I'll* work with you.'

'But your education. I mean – last time I asked you you ran away to Uncle—'

'Yeah, but I hadn't been in a house before, had I? Where is this place you're going to anyway?'

'Wales.'

There was a long silence. 'I'll miss me mates,' said Len.

'You belt up for a start,' said Reuben. 'You're the reason we're going to Wales, so get that through that thick head of yours.' He went up and rumpled Len's hair to take the sting out of his words. 'Mark you, we may bless you in the end, boy. Wales might be a right paradise.'

'Mind you come back soon,' said Vi.

'Tomorrow night,' he repeated. Then Reuben turned back to Billy. 'You mean what you said?'

'Yes, Dad.'

'That you'd come and work with me?'

'Yes, Dad.'

'And what about your education?'

'There's night school, isn't there? I've just realised something.'

'What's that?'

'It's more important to be together. Outside. Not inside.' He looked round him and shuddered. 'How can we hear the rain on the roof in here?'

'You'll hear it soon,' said Reuben reassuringly. 'We'll get back to the sounds we know. What about the wind on the heath then?'

'There's a poem about that,' said Vi, who seemed to be much more reassured now. 'There was this bloke – George something – who went travelling. He

132

was a Gorgio, mind, but he didn't half say poems well. My mum taught it to me.' She paused and then began to recite softly:

*'There's night and day, brother, both sweet things;*
*Sun, moon, and stars, brother, all sweet things;*
*There's likewise a wind on the heath.*
*Life is very sweet, brother; who would want to die?'*

There was a long silence. A tear ran down Len's cheek.

'I want to go to Wales, Dad.'

'Then I'll be off – to see if I can find somewhere.'

'What are the chances?' asked Prim.

'I've got the contacts. But I'll raise no hopes now.' He kissed them all and then walked towards the front door. 'Don't worry,' he said. 'I'll find that wind on the heath.'

'You just moved in?' The boy was about Billy's age. He was strongly built with a sulky look. Billy had seen him at school and knew him to be one of the bullies.

'Yeah. We're not staying.'

'Gypsies, aren't you?'

'Travellers.'

'Why aren't you travelling then?' His tone was mocking and Billy clenched his fists.

'We're waiting to go to Wales.'

'Aren't you the one with the horse? The black horse.'

'Yeah. How do you know?'

'Someone told me at school. You gonna bring it here?'

'No – it's with me mates.'

'Girl called Susan told me. Right snob.'

'She's a mate of me sister's. She's OK. I teach her to ride.'

'That Susan. Stuck up little creep.'

'Better not let my sister hear you say that.'

'Stuck up little creep,' shouted the boy loudly.

Prim came out into the overgrown back garden. 'What's going on?'

Billy sighed. The last thing they wanted was any more trouble. 'What's your name?' he said.

'What's it to you?' asked the boy aggressively.

'Just wondered.'

'Who's stuck up?' asked Prim.

'My name's Ted,' sneered the boy. 'I was just talking about that Susan.'

'She's my mate,' said Prim. 'She's not stuck up.'

'She is an' all.'

'You're just stupid.'

'What?'

'You must be stupid to think Susan's stuck up.'

Ted climbed over his rickety garden fence and Billy sighed again. Trouble was coming and there was nothing he could do to stop it.

'So I'm thick, am I?'

'You must be if you think Susan's stuck up. She's been learning to ride with us and I think she's great. Absolutely great. And she's my friend. So clear out of our garden.'

'You take that back.'

'About you being thick? That's hard.'

'Why?' The sneer was out of his voice and he sounded curiously disconcerted. Obviously he wasn't used to people standing up to him.

'Because you *are* thick.'

Enraged he swung at her and missed. Staggering forwards, he received the full force of Prim's fist on his chin. He went down hard on the muddy earth.

'Want some more?' asked Prim.

'Sure.' He got up and rushed at her. With yet another sigh, Billy waded in.

'I can stick up for myself,' yelled Prim angrily as he intercepted Ted's lunge.

'Don't see why I should be left out of the fun,' Billy said, swopping punches with Ted. They clinched and went down on the ground, rolling about, cursing, hitting, kicking – but not doing much damage to each other. Then, just as Billy was getting on top, someone else sprang over the fence. This time it was a large man who looked very much like Ted except that his chin was covered in shaving cream and he was wearing old trousers, a vest, pair of braces and carpet slippers. He pulled Billy and Ted apart, holding them away from each other.

'Gypos,' he said. 'I knew there'd be trouble once you lot moved in.'

'It wasn't us – it was him,' yelled Prim. 'He called my mate stuck up.'

'So you have to belt him, do you?'

135

'He tried to slap her,' said Billy. 'And she hit him.'

'Did she now – the little madam.' The man glared at them both while Ted, panting and filthy, looked pleased.

'Oi – you leave my brother alone.' Len strode out into the back garden, followed by his mother.

'Quiet you,' she said. 'Now just what's going on?'

'They started on my Ted.'

'Rubbish.' Prim was briskly dismissive. 'He jumped over the fence.'

'You been fighting, Bill?' asked Len admiringly. 'Who won?'

'Be quiet.' Vi pushed Len into the background. 'I don't want another word out of you.'

'But, Mum—'

'Or there'll be another fight. Between you and me. And I don't have to tell you who will win that. Do I, Len?'

'No, Mum.'

'Now – we don't want to be bad neighbours,' said Vi, 'so why don't I make a cup of tea—'

'Get over that fence, Ted,' said his father. 'We don't want to talk to the likes of them.'

'Gypos,' muttered Ted.

But Vi was too quick for him to make his exit. '*What* did you say, son?'

'Nothing.'

But she had already grabbed him – and was shaking Ted as hard as she could. 'Did you say "gypos"?'

'No.'

'I heard you say it.'

'Leave my son alone.'

'When he learns some manners.'

'Madam—'

'Mum, leave him,' said Prim.

Vi pushed Ted away. 'Take him back,' she said, half sobbing. 'We don't want him here.'

Unexpectedly the man's eyes softened. 'Look – there's no need to get so upset.'

'If my husband was here – he wouldn't let you treat me like this.'

'I'm not treating you like anything.'

'He'd soon sort you out.'

'Madam—'

'Mum, give over,' said Billy. 'Dad'll be back tomorrow night.'

'He shouldn't have left me in this place.' She was really sobbing now. 'This wouldn't have happened if we was outdoors—'

'Come on, Mum,' said Prim, putting her arm round her mother's waist. 'Let's go in and have a cuppa – and Len, you come with us.'

'No.'

'Len!' roared Vi through her tears. 'Do what she says.'

Ted and his dad climbed over the fence. Billy couldn't work out whether they were ashamed or not. But what had really shocked him was Mum – she seemed all broken up.

*

137

Vi had just settled down again when there was a knock on the door.

'Now what?' said Len. 'Another fight?'

Billy went to the door. There was another very large man standing outside in a T-shirt, despite the cold. He had tattoos up both arms but there was a kind, considerate look in his eye.

'Hi.' His voice was warm.

'Yeah?' Billy wasn't being too friendly, especially with Mum the way she was.

'Can I see your mum?'

'What do you want?'

'I'm your next-door neighbour – the other side.'

'Something wrong?'

'No. I was going to drop in to say hello anyway. Couldn't help but hear what went on in your back garden, so thought I'd come in right away. I just wanted to say that we're not all like that on this estate.'

'Who's that?' shouted Vi.

'Chris Greenaway – your *friendly* next-door neighbour.'

'Come on in.'

Vi was in a bad way when he came in – a mood that Prim and the boys had never seen her in before. She seemed desperate, and quite unable to cope. He shook hands with her.

'You upset, missus?'

'I'm surrounded by it—'

'Don't start *again*, Mum,' said Prim as the tears ran down her mother's cheeks and the sobs renewed.

'I can't help it. They *all* hate Travellers up here. Call us "gypos". Start my Billy fighting. And he never fights.'

'Doesn't he?' asked Len but she ignored him.

'I belted that Ted,' said Prim indignantly, but Vi ignored her too.

'Some of my best mates are Travellers,' said Chris. 'I work up in the scrapyard in town. Lever Brothers. We see a lot of Travellers in our trade. I mean, it's your trade too, isn't it? What's your name, missus?'

'Vi Roberts. My husband's gone to look for a new site – miles away in Wales. We got nowhere else to go now – and we don't like houses.'

'I know you don't. When you going to Wales?'

'Day after tomorrow,' she said firmly. 'Can't stand any more of it here.'

'Pity – thought we might be friends.' He paused. 'Working the way I do, somehow I feel more like a Traveller than a Gorgio. Got used to being with 'em.'

Vi sniffed. 'Get some tea on, Billy. Give the gentleman some tea.'

'OK, Mum.'

'Thanks. Don't judge us all by the Harlows.'

'Them lot? Ted's lot?'

'He's uncouth he is – they all are. Poor little sod.'

'Ted?'

'Yeah, his old man's up for battering him – and his mum.'

'Ted's a bully,' stated Billy tersely.

'Yeah. He passes it on, don't he? He's covered in

bruises from that old man of his. Welfare been up. Poor kid, he ain't got no mates either.'

'He called us gypos,' said Billy, passing Chris a cup of tea. 'We won't have it.'

'He gets it from his dad.'

'Why doesn't his dad like us?' asked Billy.

'Maybe because you're free,' replied Chris. 'It gets him unsettled like.'

'We're not free,' said Vi. 'We're prisoners, that's what we are.'

'It's bad about Ted.' Prim was really worried. 'Can't we do something to stop his old man beating him?'

'We tried everything. They got a social worker now. But he still goes on knocking him about.'

There was a long pause. Then Chris said, 'When does your husband get back?'

'Tomorrow night,' said Vi. 'And then we're off, or at least I hope to God we are. Back in the trailer.'

'First time you been in a house?'

'Yes. I'll never sleep.'

'Would you like to sleep in a tent? Just for a night?'

'A tent?' Vi was doubtful. 'Bit chilly.'

'Not mine – army surplus. Beautifully warm. I can lend you a little calor gas heater *and* a light.'

'That sounds great, Mum,' said Len.

'Camping in November?' She shook her head. 'I don't know.'

'There've been Travellers here before,' said Chris. 'Moved in on this estate. Never could settle. Never could sleep the first night. It's not the first time my tent's been used for this purpose.' He beamed at them proudly. 'Give it a swing, missus.'

'It's good of you—'

'Say yes, Mum,' insisted Prim. 'It's only for the night. And if Dad – when Dad gets back – we'll be off in the truck. So we can safely say we *never* slept in a house. How about that, Mum? They won't have beaten us after all.'

'All right,' said Vi. 'At least we'll be out of doors.' She looked up at the ceiling. 'I'm like my Billy – I'd feel the weight of that ceiling pressing on me all night.'

While Chris was getting the tent, Billy wandered out into the garden again. Casually he strolled along by the low fence and caught sight of Ted reading a comic in the garden shed. Billy whistled and Ted looked up. Slowly, he put down the comic and came out.

'Want to finish that fight,' he leered. 'Want me to beat you in?'

Billy shook his head. 'Thought you might like to play football.'

'Where?'

'Down the road. There's a bit of a green. I got a new football.'

'What you want to play with me for?'

'Thought we could be mates. Just for tonight. We gotta go tomorrow. After school.'

'To Wales?'

141

'Yeah.'

Ted nodded. 'I'll come. Me dad's gone out.' He climbed back over the fence.

'Come round the side,' said Billy. 'My sister's in the house.'

'I'm not scared of your sister.'

'Only joking.'

Billy led him round the side. At the front they met Chris, lugging in part of the tent.

'Me and Ted's going to knock the ball about.'

Chris grinned.

Ted and Billy had a good time kicking the football about. Some other kids joined in and there was no trouble with anyone. But just as they were finishing the game, Mr Harlow strode down the road.

'Oi – Ted.'

Ted looked up and immediately Billy could see the fear in his eyes.

'I told you what would happen if you were late for your tea again. You're gonna get it.'

Mr Harlow walked up to his son and gave him a terrific slap round the head. Ted fell over on the grass, and all the other kids moved away. Except Billy.

'That's not right,' he said.

'What?' Mr Harlow was very red in the face. 'Who you think you're talking to then?'

'He's smaller than you,' Billy continued shakily.

'So are you, Gypo. Now unless you want more of the same, clear off.'

142

'Ted got to his feet. 'It's all right, Bill.'

'But he shouldn't be hitting you like that.'

'He's my dad,' said Ted defensively.

'What?'

'He's my dad – and he does what he likes. Get it?'

'Yeah.'

'And it's none of your business. Right?'

'Right.'

'Come on then,' said Mr Harlow in a softer voice. 'Let's get some tea.'

They walked away side by side, with Billy staring at them in consternation. Then a small girl came up to him. She spoke like an adult.

'He's loyal, that Ted.'

'Yeah.'

'He won't have a word said against his dad. But they're coming for him tomorrow.'

'Who?'

'The Welfare. Ted's going into care.'

Billy walked slowly back home. He didn't understand Gorgio ways and he didn't want to. Of course Dad belted him from time to time and he knew other Travellers' dads belted their kids even harder. But to go into care . . . It didn't bear thinking about. That was a Gorgio way. It had to be.

# 11    *On the Road Again*

'Dad!' Billy shouted with joy.

Reuben stood on the doorstep. It was just after eight. He looked worn out.

'I got us a site.'

'No.'

'I did an' all. And Silas and me got the trailers all hitched up. He brought me over in his motor. We've even got Blackie in the back of the truck – all fixed up with hay and a stall.'

Silas waved from his battered estate car.

'You mean—'

'We're on the road again.'

'Great!'

'Where's Mum?'

'In her tent.'

'In her *what*?'

'Bloke next door lent us a tent. Mum thought the ceiling was coming down.'

'Probably will – in a dump like this. Go and get the others.'

'Don't you want to rest?'

'Not in here. We'll pull over somewhere about midnight.'

Billy rushed out and collected Mum, Prim and Len. They were overjoyed to see Reuben.

'Didn't you trust me?' he asked as he embraced Vi.

'Give over. I don't know what to think these days. What's the new site like then?'

'It's fantastic. In the mountains.'

'And who owns it?'

'No one.'

'So who says we can go there?'

'The Bensons.'

'Jack and Ivy?'

'Yeah. There's a load of Travellers there. It's unofficial but they're never hassled. Maybe one day – but we stand more of a chance up there, Vi. It's Travellers' country.'

'And what's that supposed to mean?'

'You can smell the wind on the heath.'

'Give over.'

'It's true. And we'll get in on the breaking. No likely partners. But I've got one now. You still on, Bill?'

'I'm still on, Dad.'

'Let's get going then.'

Chris came down his garden path with his young wife. 'This is Betty,' he said. 'You off then?'

'You the gentleman who lent the wife and kids a tent?'

'Yeah.'

145

'Thanks a lot.'

'Got your place then?'

'Yeah. We gotta get going.'

'Dad—'

'Yes, Bill?'

'Can I say goodbye to a mate?'

'If you're quick.'

'He's only next door.' Billy walked over to the front door of Ted's home and knocked. His mother opened the door, a harried, miserable-looking woman.

'What do you want?'

'Ted.'

'I don't know if he's in.'

'I am, Mum.' He came running to the door. 'I'm in.' He pushed past her to Billy. He looked pale and drawn. 'I thought you were the . . .' Then he stopped and changed what he was going to say. 'You off, then?'

'Just came to say goodbye. I'd like to have been mates for longer.'

'So would I,' said Ted. 'I'm sorry about—'

'It doesn't matter.'

Ted looked across at Prim. 'You pack a punch.'

Prim smiled. 'I've got to stick up for our lot.'

'I think gyp – Travellers – are great, Mum.'

'You come in now.'

'Where you going?'

'Wales.'

'Is it far?'

146

'Yeah. If you're ever in Wales,' said Billy generously, 'drop in for a cup of tea.'

'I will,' said Ted.

'Come on *in* now,' snapped his mother. 'Your dad'll be back in a minute – and I don't know *what* he'll say.'

'I do,' Ted replied grimly. He put out his hand. 'Shake?' He looked close to tears.

'OK,' said Billy.

'What about you?' Ted asked Prim.

'Sure.' She came and shook his hand – and Len raced up to do the same.

'What did you call us?' Len asked with his usual total lack of tact. 'I can't think what it was now – you know – that caused the fight and all.'

'Shut up, Len,' said Prim.

'Better get going.' Dad looked at his watch.

'Bye, Ted. See you.' Billy grinned. Then he turned to Chris and Betty. 'And if you're ever in Wales,' he said grandly, 'do drop in as well.'

Reuben drove the truck and Mum the van, each with a trailer behind. They went slowly in convoy along the motorway and after a brief rest kept moving all the way through a cold and rainy night. Billy was amazed to see how well his dad coped with the long drive when he was already so tired, but fell asleep himself before he could really start worrying about him.

When he woke, Billy saw the most amazing sight.

They were on a very high bridge and surging along below them was a huge river, its waters green and winking. Frost covered the banks, shining like jewels.

'Where are we, Dad?'

'Severn Bridge.'

'Hey, look at that!'

In front of them was an extraordinary double decker bus. It was covered in the most amazing drawings – mainly eyes. And in the pupils of the eyes there were all kinds of different weird scenes – sunrises and sunsets, seascapes and fantastic cities. Then Billy heard the sound of a police siren and a police car roared up behind them as they came off the bridge. The man behind the wheel kept signalling them in to the side. Then he overhauled them and signalled the bus in to the side as well.

'Everybody out,' the policeman said, while his two colleagues ran up and down knocking at the windows of the bus and the truck and the van.

'What's up?' asked Reuben.

'You'll see,' said one of the policemen. 'Everybody out.'

Two men with beards and tunics, two women with long dresses and half a dozen very young children clambered out of the bus. They all looked very weary but quite calm, while the Roberts were distinctly nervous.

'All right, you lot. No one's going any further,' rasped the policeman who seemed to be spokesman.

'Why not?' said Reuben, bewildered. 'We got a pitch to go to.'

'Have you now? We don't want the Convoy round here, see.'

'Convoy? What convoy?'

'You hippy bunch of trouble-makers,' continued the policeman.

'We're Travellers,' said Vi. 'Not hippies.'

'Travellers, hippies – they're all the same. We've got instructions—'

'Wait a minute.' One of the bearded men spoke quietly. 'I think you're making a mistake, officer.'

'Oh yes? What kind of mistake?' said the policeman truculently.

'Well, we're not the same at all. We're hippies; they're gypsies.' He turned apologetically to Reuben. 'I know you don't like that term, but I don't think this officer understands the word Traveller.'

'Then who are you – you hippies then?' asked Reuben, confused.

'We're Travellers too in a way. We've just dropped out of society and travel around – if we're allowed to.'

The policeman whispered something to a colleague and all three of them had a flurried conversation. Then the spokesman turned back to Reuben. 'Do you have a licence and insurance papers?'

'I'll get them, Dad,' volunteered Billy. He went to the front of the truck and got them out. 'You'll find them all in order,' he said, passing them over.

'He your secretary?' grinned the policeman.

'Eh?'

He flicked through the documents and then handed them back.

'Going far, sir?'

'Radich.'

'Oh yes – what's in the truck?'

'A horse.'

'No horse-box, sir?'

'We use the truck – it's adapted.'

One of the policemen wandered round the back and peered inside. He returned, apparently satisfied. 'It's OK,' he announced.

'Well, you'd better be on your way, sir.'

'I don't understand,' said Reuben. 'Why've you stopped these people? They haven't done anything.'

'We don't know about that yet, sir.'

'But—'

'And I wouldn't advise you to get involved, sir. We stopped you by mistake, thinking you were part of this outfit. We're sorry if we inconvenienced you, but now you must be on your way.'

'I still don't see what they've—'

One of the bearded men stepped forward and put his hand on Reuben's arm. 'Please don't get involved on our behalf, friend. We don't want you to get into trouble. You're the original Travellers – you still have your freedom.'

'What about yours?'

'We have to fight every inch of the way for ours. You Romanies – you've got the tradition.'

'If people want to travel—' began Reuben indignantly.

'Come on, love,' said Vi, who could see the look in the policeman's eyes. 'Let's get going.'

'She's right,' said one of the women from the bus. 'Please go. The longer you stay, the more difficult it'll be for you. But we do appreciate your concern.'

'Now, stop arguing the toss and get on your way.'

Still indignant, Reuben climbed into the driver's seat of the truck and Vi went back into the van. They pulled back on to the road again, leaving the policemen examining the bus with vigorous enthusiasm. One of the hippies raised an arm in resigned farewell.

'It's miles from anywhere.'

'That's what we want.'

'Can they get the telly?'

'What about the shops?'

'It's a wilderness.'

The hills were long and rolling, with close-cropped grass and a sky that seemed much bigger than anything they had seen in the south. The Roberts had got out of the vehicles to look down into the dark steep-sided valley. It looked different, mysterious. Smoke curled up from the trailers – there must have been a couple of dozen of them – and there was the thin outline of a tumbling rocky stream running past the camp.

'It's a real camp,' said Prim, expressing everyone's thoughts exactly. 'Not a site.'

'Have we come home?' asked Vi.

'What do you mean, Mum?' Len was puzzled.

She shook her head. 'I don't know what I mean.'

'Blackie will love it here. Dad, can I ride him down there?'

'Well . . .'

'I can see a track. We can make it.'

'OK, boy – ride him.'

They backed a reluctant Blackie out of the truck. 'Don't saddle him up,' said Billy. 'I want to ride him bareback.'

'You'll have a sore bum,' warned Vi.

'It'll give me the feel of the place,' said Billy.

They watched Blackie pick his way cautiously down the steep track. Soon rider and horse became smaller and smaller.

'He looks real fine,' said Reuben. 'Like he's riding into a new land.'

'Yes,' said Vi briskly. 'But what's our reception going to be like?' There was fear in her voice. 'Are they friendly?'

'Yes,' said Reuben. 'They're friendly.'

'Guarantee that?'

'Yeah.'

'And what are the catches? There must be catches.'

'It's no paradise. It's a barren land. I can join up with some car breakers, but it might not pay enough. It's not an official site – but no one's been moved on for years. Mind you, with our luck—'

'It's eviction tomorrow.'

'Those are the catches. Enough for you?'

'They'll do.' Vi took Reuben's hand. 'It's like we've emigrated.'

'Eh?'

'Come to a new land. Like you said with Billy.'

'It's a new land all right. Maybe a new life.'

'There wasn't a lot wrong with the old life,' said Vi. 'Except moving on.'

'You gonna be all right, you two?' demanded Len.

Reuben breathed in the afternoon air and put his other arm round Len.

'Come here, Prim love,' said Vi. 'I want to hold you.'

They all stood arm in arm, hand in hand, looking down at the darkening twilight of the smoky valley. A light came on in a trailer. A dog barked. A child called out.

'Let's go,' said Reuben.

Slowly Prim followed. Was it going to be a new life? Well, there would be a new school. But after that she faced a future of helping Mum and waiting for a bloke. Did she really want that, she wondered. In her heart of hearts she knew she didn't.

Looking down as she walked, Prim saw a long line of small clothes stretching from a trailer to a tree. A young girl was pegging up some more, and even from this distance Prim could see she was heavily pregnant.

And yet, as she gradually drew nearer, she could smell the woodsmoke, bacon frying, the tang of the earth. That was the Travellers' way of life. She loved these smells – they were freedom – but she must never forget that for her they could also be a prison. She plunged on, more quickly now. 'Wait for me,' she called after them.

# PLAYING WITH FIRE
## *Anthony Masters*

The new St Elmer's Primary School has been built on the site of an ancient abbey, and everyone is talking about the monks who used to live there. Will their ghosts be found sitting at spare desks at the back of the class?

Of course, no one really believes any of the silly rumours, but when term begins, the teachers begin to behave very oddly. Chris and Tim are determined to uncover the truth behind some of the peculiar goings-on.
A humorous mystery story with a slightly sinister edge.

# ESIO TROT
## *Roald Dahl*

Mr Hoppy is in love with Mrs Silver. But Mrs Silver has eyes only for Alfie, her pet tortoise. How can he ever compete with such a rival? He comes up with a bold plan to win his lady's love, involving some clever riddles and a whole army of tortoises. Will Mr Hoppy's patience be rewarded? And what's to become of Alfie?

A highly comic and unusual love story.

# JUST FERRET
## *Gene Kemp*

Owen Hardacre, otherwise known as Ferret, has been dragged around the country by his artist father and been to so many schools that he doesn't expect much from Cricklepit Combined School. But when he makes friends with Beany and Minty and gains the respect of Sir, things begin looking up ... even the reading!

Meet Ferret, his friends *and* enemies in this fifth story of the pupils of Cricklepit Combined School.

## STORMSEARCH
### Robert Westall

It is Tim who finds the model ship buried in the sand and, with growing excitement, he, his sister Tracey and their eccentric Uncle Geoff realize the significance of their discovery. For the model ship yields up a long-forgotten secret and a story of danger and romance.

## THE WATER HORSE
### Dick King-Smith

Last night's storm has washed up a strange object like a giant mermaid's purse, which Kirstie takes home and puts in the bath. The next day it has hatched into a tiny greeny-grey creature, with a horse's head, a warty skin, four flippers and a crocodile's tail. The adorable baby sea monster soon becomes the family pet – but the trouble is, he just doesn't stop growing!

## MAN IN MOTION
### Jan Mark

His sister had had friends round. How had she managed to make so many so fast? Once Lloyd has started at his new school, however, he soon finds he's playing cricket with Salman, swimming with Kenneth, cycling with James and playing badminton with Vlad. But American football is Lloyd's greatest enthusiasm, and in time it tests his loyalties, not only to his other sporting activities, but also to the new friends he shares them with.

# FLOWER OF JET
## Bell Mooney

It's the time of the miners' strike. Tom Farrell's father is branded with the word Tom most dreads; Melanie Wall's father is the strike leader. How can Tom and Melanie's friendship survive the violence and bitterness of both sides? Things are to grow far worse than they ever imagined, for Melanie and Tom discover a treacherous plot that could destroy both their families. And they have to act fast if they're going to stop it.

# MIGHTIER THAN THE SWORD
## Clare Bevan

Adam had always felt he was somehow special, different from the rest of the family, but could he really be a modern-day King Arthur, the legendary figure they're learning about at school? Inspired by the stories they are hearing in class, Adam and his friends become absorbed in a complex game of knights and good deeds. All they need is a worthy cause for which to fight. So when they discover that the local pond is under threat, Adam's knights are ready to join battle with the developers.

Reality and legend begin to blur in this lively, original story about an imaginative boy who doesn't let a mere wheelchair get in his way of adventure.

# AGAINST THE STORM
## Gaye Hicyilmaz

'As Mehmet is drawn into his parents' ill-considered scheme to go and live in Ankara, the directness and the acute observation of Gaye Hicyilmaz carry the reader with him ... Terrible things happen: illness, humiliation, death. But Mehmet is a survivor, and as the book closes, 'a sort of justice' has been done, and a satisfying victory achieved. It is a sort of justice too ... that in all the dire traffic of unpublishable manuscripts something as fresh and powerful as this should emerge' – *The Times*